BR

Crossing into strike force "greened up," meaning that all switches were set for ordnance release. The Thuds and Phantoms turned and chased their shadows down Thud Ridge, as the North Vietnamese gunners attempted to lock them in their sights. But seeing such fast-moving targets was one thing—shooting them down was another.

At the eastern end of Thud Ridge, the mighty bridge was clearly visible against a backdrop of Red River currents. Rolling in, the F-105 pilots saw the flak suppressor ships going to work and an 85mm site simply disappear in a massive explosion north of the river.

In each cockpit the stick was pushed forward. Instrument dials whirled as the nose of every plane dropped. It took about seven seconds to complete the dive, seven seconds that seemed like seven days in that welter of exploding steel ...

☆

WRECKING CREW

WRECKING CREW:

THE 388TH TACTICAL FIGHTER WING IN VIETNAM

JERRY SCUTTS

WARNER BOOKS

A Warner Communications Company

WARNER BOOKS EDITIONS

Cover photo by U.S. Air Force
Cover design by Don Puckey

Warner Books, Inc.
666 Fifth Avenue
New York, N.Y. 10103

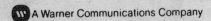 A Warner Communications Company

Printed in the United States of America

First Printing: July, 1990

10 9 8 7 6 5 4 3 2 1

I N August 1945, as their comrades in arms prepared to deliver the knockout blow to the Japanese Empire, the men of the Allied 8th Air Force's 388th Bomb Group arrived back in the United States from England for deactivation. Its work as a 3rd Division B-17 group over, the 388th stood down on 28 August. Time passed and the old Army Air Forces slipped into history with the formation of a separate United States Air Force in September 1947.

Some six years later, with the Korean War virtually over, the 388th unit number returned to the rolls of the Air Force as a day fighter wing based at Clovis Air Force Base, New Mexico. From 23 March 1953, the 388th Wing had three squadrons assigned—the 561st, 562nd and 563rd—jet fighter units using the same numbering as three out of four of the 388th Bomb Group's squadrons. Only the 560th had gone.

It was the following year before aircraft, in the shape of the F-86 Sabre, arrived to equip the Wing. As was usual USAF practice, the new 388th Fighter Bomber Wing inherited the history and honors of the bomb group that had flown against Germany out of Knettishall, UK.

Europe was soon to become more than just a collection of place names in the records to Wing personnel, as in November 1954 the 388th shipped out, destination France.

Under NATO agreements, the Wing became part of United States Air Forces Europe and based its Sabres at Etain/Rouvres, a short distance from historic Verdun. The Wing flew F and H model F-86s until late 1956, when something more potent and better able to handle a possible threat from the east appeared on the scene—the F-100 Super Sabre. Both single-seat D and two-seat F model Huns were operated by the 388th during its time in Europe.

It was during its tour in USAFE that the 388th Wing's badge was approved, on 11 March 1955. Consisting of a shield with three diagonal segments colored dark blue, white, and yellow reading from the top, there was a black lightning flash across the center. The shield surmounted a white scroll, which contained the Wing's motto, LIBERTAS VEL MORS (Liberty or Death), in black capital letters. As originally drawn, the whole device was supported by a pair of light blue wings, but these were subsequently deleted.

Rationalization of NATO-USAF forces brought a number of changes in 1957, with the result that the 388th was a Super Sabre outfit for less than one year. On 10

December, it was deactivated and the 49th TFW absorbed most of its assets, including aircraft.

The third reactivation occurred on 1 May 1962, when the 388th Tactical Fighter Wing established its base at McConnell AFB, Kansas. New F-105 Thunderchiefs joined F-100s for a training stint lasting approximately two years. On 8 February 1964, the 388th was absorbed by the 23rd TFW at McConnell.

By that time, events in Southeast Asia had led to a significant US presence in South Vietnam and neighboring Thailand. Since April 1961, the Air Force had had a control and reporting center at Don Muang airport in Thailand, and had based F-102 interceptors and RF-101 reconnaissance aircraft there on a temporary-duty basis. While the Delta Daggers undertook a passive, local defense duty in company with the Royal Thai Air Force, the Voodoos carried out a number of recon sorties over Laos to keep a watch on the supply lines for Hanoi-backed Vietcong insurgents operating in South Vietnam.

While the United States continued to train and equip the small South Vietnamese Air Force to make more effective use of airpower against an elusive, well-organized and -supplied enemy, the political effort to give the South stable government progressed in the face of considerable internal strife, particularly from Buddhist factions that suffered government repression.

The US believed that it was necessary to have a Vietnamese administration that was both popular and strongly resolved to committing its own ground and air forces fully to stop Vietcong insurgency before providing significant military backing—and certainly before American nationals became involved in the war on any scale, whether they be ground troops or aircrew. In the meantime the buildup proceeded at a slow pace, the rotation of TAC squadrons into Thailand being at little more strength than normal overseas deployment by the USAF anywhere else in the world.

But in August 1964, the picture changed radically. Following the attack by North Vietnamese gunboats on destroyers of the Seventh Fleet, Congress adopted the Tonkin Gulf Resolution, giving President Lyndon Johnson wide-ranging powers to respond to attacks on US forces and retaliate against North Vietnam's continuing aggression in the South. However, every effort was made to play down the US involvement in the Southeast Asian conflict, particularly the possibility of the aircraft in Thailand flying strike missions into the North. For a few more months it would remain only a possibility, the early retaliatory air strikes being mounted by the Navy and SVNAF. As an insurance, the Joint Chiefs of Staff (JCS) drew up a list of ninety-four potential targets in North Vietnam and, not unreasonably, presented a case for a rapid, all-out series of air strikes that would have crippled the North's economy and her war-making potential.

Johnson's view of the war—and more significantly, perhaps, that of the Secretary of Defense Robert S. McNamara—did not gel with those of the service chiefs. Johnson clung to the belief that so awesome was the very threat of massive US intervention in the war, particularly the deployment of her airpower, that no nation on earth would be foolhardy enough to resist. A study of history—and very recent history at that—should have told him otherwise.

Johnson feared Chinese intervention in the conflict at a time when North Vietnam and China were not on the best of terms, and he misread the tenacity of Ho Chi Minh's regime to fulfill a pledge to reunite Vietnam under the banner of communism at almost any cost. From the start, when this tiny, backward nation showed little or no sign of being cowed by US might, the White House created a highly optimistic vision of the war, far removed from the battlefield in a great deal more than distance; if anything, Johnson saw the conflict as another Korea. There were indeed similarities, but as far as actual events transpired, that is what they remained.

Not that Johnson's view of the power of American arms was an isolated view. Many decision-makers shared it. But in so doing, they overlooked the fact that in every previous war, the gloves had been off. American military forces had been free, against a defined enemy and under a declaration of war, to field as much firepower as was necessary until a conclusion—invariably victory—was achieved. This time, things were going to be appallingly different. Politically, Johnson's "short war" would have been acceptable, but militarily it was a disaster. The Germans proved in Europe in World War II that it was indeed possible to achieve victory in the space of a few weeks. The United States tried to do much the same thing in Vietnam—but without the Blitzkrieg or the key element of an invasion by ground forces.

While the Chiefs of Staff, the President, and his advisers deliberated over how they should handle the conflict they had been drawn into, events in Vietnam showed little sign of improvement. Terrorist bombs in Saigon killed and injured Americans in December 1964, and in

February 1965 the Vietcong attacked the US base at
Pleiku. The latter event was the last straw; most members
of the National Security Council now recommended as-
sertive US air action against the North. Accordingly, the
Navy struck the Dong Hoi barracks just north of the
Demilitarized Zone on 7 February.

A short series of ''Flaming Dart'' air strikes followed,
and from then on, the onus was placed on airpower to
do something it had never before been asked to do
alone—namely, to achieve victory over the enemy.
Without a recognized declaration of war, lacking United
Nations support, and with a civilian stranglehold on what
targets it should hit, when it should hit them, and even
what ordnance it should use in the process, the United
States sent the Air Force into action over North Vietnam.

The F-100, F-102, amd F-104 lacked the performance
and load-carrying capability to fly strike missions against
North Vietnam's increasingly deadly ground defenses.
Tactical Air Command therefore had only the F-105
available in sufficient numbers to carry out the task. Super
Sabres and Starfighters would subsequently fly frequently
over North Vietnam, but in roles other than bombing.

The US considered its best course attacking North Vietnam's industrial base, a process that wasted many
months. And the potential targets for air attack were
surrounded by an array of antiaircraft artillery weapons
supplied, in the main, by the Soviet Union and China.
Concurrently, an intensive program of training gunners
and radar operators was initiated.

US intelligence estimated that the primary targets were
defended by guns ranging in caliber from 12.7mm to

100mm, the majority of the larger ones with radar ranging. Figures for August 1964 put the total at 1,426 guns, 22 early-warning radars, and four fire-control radars. In addition, North Vietnam mobilized its population to defend the country against air attack using any weapon available. US air strikes would have to contend not only with heavier-caliber AAA in the immediate target areas, but a veritable wall of small-arms fire on most ingress and egress routes.

Fortunately the F-105 was a tough, Mach 2–plus fighter bomber well able to sustain damage and bring its pilot home safely. It relied on an impressive turn of speed at low altitude—indeed there were few aircraft anywhere that could touch a Thud in afterburner piling on the coals down in the weeds. What worried squadron commanders was the F-105's poor reliability record prior to its appearance in Thailand; for every flying hour, an excessive period of ground maintenance had been required, making the aircraft hardly an economical proposition.

But with great support from the manufacturer and service maintenance teams, the Thud and its systems stood up to the harsh environmental conditions of Thailand extremely well. And as the first operational sorties were flown, it showed itself well able to take battle damage in all but a few vital areas.

Combat flying in Vietnam was no different from that in other wars in that the first participants had almost to start from scratch as far as tactics were concerned. Peacetime deployment of the Thunderchief and other TAC fighters during the late 1950s and early 1960s gave little heed to ground attack. The emphasis had been heavily on the interception of bombers and the ''once and for all'' delivery of tactical nuclear weapons. The squadrons tasked with operational duty in Thailand adapted previous deployment doctrine to the ''old-fashioned'' delivery of iron bombs on a variety of targets under a very limited degree of in-theater flexibility. On paper, no flexibility existed at all.

The tortuous chain of command, stretching all the way from the Oval Office to flight operations at the Thai bases, did unfortunately contain a number of links who were totally out of touch with modern tactical airpower. The post–World War II Air Force had seen the elevation to command positions of many ''bomber men'' who often saw the war in Strategic Air Command terms—which still included high-altitude straight and level bomb-on-command sorties that took no account of the advantages possessed by fighters. Such was the hold these individuals had over junior officers, despite the latter's considerable fighter experience, that there were few men who dared to impose their own techniques on their pilots for fear of reprimand—or worse. Not surprisingly, TAC units in Thailand began to sustain losses when their field orders were carried out to the letter.

In order to blunt the flow of supplies to communist forces operating in the South, a great many targets briefed for the strike squadrons in Thailand were small, difficult to hit, and heavily defended. The weather also played a significant part. Hot, humid, and very often covered by a thick blanket of cloud, Vietnam is a country where planning an air campaign over a sustained period of time has to allow very much for prevailing weather conditions, particularly during the monsoon season from December to June, which can hide potential targets for days at a time. While US aircraft could rely heavily on radar acquisition of targets, the restrictions of the self-imposed "rules of engagement" often prevented an attack going ahead unless visibility was ideal. And the advantages of good weather were, of course, available to the defenders in equal measure.

But under all these difficulties, the US began flying sorties and working down the modified list of targets drawn up thousands of miles away from the scene of the action. Airmen knew (as they had always known) that a target damaged one day would only be posted on the board for a repeat strike the next. Therefore, every effort was made to put the bombs on the bridge, factory, or vehicle assembly point so that it could, if only for a short period, be struck off. Few targets attacked in the early days could actually be struck off, such was the North Vietnamese skill and courage in making good the damage inflicted or bypassing it in order to keep the men and materiel rolling southward.

Under these conditions, the US opened the joint Air Force–Navy campaign on northern targets known as "Rolling Thunder" on 2 March 1965. North Vietnam showed no indication of having noticed the fact, or of being unduly worried about the implications, although in March and April of that year there was a lower level of Vietcong activity in the South than hitherto.

For the purposes of the Rolling Thunder campaign, North Vietnam was divided into a number of areas, known as Route Packs I to VI. This simplified the location of targets in a country peppered with hard-to-pronounce place names and soon served as an instant aide memoir as to how heavy the defenses might be in a given area.

The higher the route pack numbers, the nearer the target would be to Hanoi and its ring of guns.

The numbers I through IV indicated the southernmost part of North Vietnam, above the 17th parallel, where targets could be expected to be less heavily defended than the capital and its major port of Haiphong. It was in these lower route packs that pilots new to combat flying from Thailand flew their first ten missions. When he was deemed ready to undertake something a little more challenging, the rookie would be briefed on the excitement awaiting him in Route Packs V (west) and VI (east), which were as far north as US aircraft were permitted to go before coming up against an off-limits buffer zone with Red China.

On the 2 March strike, a force consisting of F-100s, B-57s, and twenty-five F-105Ds from the 18th TFW, hit an ammunition depot at Xom Bong, about thirty-five miles above the so-called demilitarized zone (DMZ) dividing the two Vietnams. As a portent of things to come, five aircraft were lost to ground fire.

On that date, the USAF had 150 F-105Ds available for combat missions in Thailand. The aircraft was rapidly building a reputation for reliability under the harshest of combat conditions. The pattern of temporary-duty rotations into Thailand was to last into 1966, when the 388th became one of two wings—the other being the 355th—that would control and coordinate the majority of operations against North Vietnam until nearly the end of US involvement in the early 1970s.

In the meantime, provisional wings directed the rotational units, which, considering the high intensity of strike missions, completed record numbers of sorties in a matter of months, their Thuds clocking up thousands of flying hours attacking radar sites, bridges, ammunition dumps, tunnels, and surface-to-air (SAM) missile sites.

This raising of the stakes by the North Vietnamese caused no little concern in the Pentagon, not to mention the briefing rooms at Korat and Takhali. Coupled with the fact that the enemy was now in a position to challenge US air strikes with a force of MiGs, the SAM threat loomed large in mission planning. It would be a factor to contend with for the rest of the war.

The MiG threat was more quantifiable. Modest in numbers, the enemy air force rarely provided the chance for decisive aerial combat, the North Vietnamese preferring to adopt hit-and-run tactics against invariably superior American formations. Their job was to reduce the weight of bombs on targets. If an aggressive move followed by a swift breakaway was all that was required for one or more F-105s to jettison their bombs, some success had been achieved. But an unladen Thud was a formidable adversary even against a well-armed MiG-17. Overall, American losses caused by MiGs were light.

The first F-105s lost to MiGs were Korat-based aircraft flying a mission on 4 April 1965. It was seen that increasing activity by the NVAF could weaken a strike force (which had enough to do against ground defenses in the target areas), and the planners realized that some form of escort had to be provided. Fortunately, that duty could be undertaken by the F-4 Phantom, the first of which arrived in Thailand in the spring of 1965.

While more sophisticated forms of deceiving the enemy as to the size of a US strike force and its intended target on a given mission were awaiting their combat

debut, a coat of paint would help immediately. From the
start of the war, USAF aircraft in Thailand had been
silver, with color trim.

In order to reduce the visibility of combat aircraft in
air-to-air encounters, paint patterns were drawn up for a
three-tone "Southeast Asia" camouflage scheme. This
was to be applied to all aircraft in the combat zones as
soon as practicable; the job was usually carried out when
an aircraft went into the shops for major overhaul. Naturally, it took time to paint every operational aircraft on
a large base, and for many months, strike squadrons went
north in aircraft in both the old and new color schemes.
The paint used did not at first take well to the conditions
and often flaked. But it was improved.

There was also the problem of recognizing aircraft
from the component squadrons of different wings while
a mission was in progress. Therefore, the next move was
to introduce a system of two-letter codes for application
to the fin of each aircraft. But it was some time before
this was done.

2

AS the war against North Vietnam gradually escalated through 1965, US strike squadrons began to find out a number of disturbing facts concerning their tactics, their weapons, and their support services. As airmen had discovered in previous conflicts, the young F-105 pilots found bridges one of the most difficult targets to knock down. Some, like the infamous "Dragon's Jaw" and the Paul Doumer bridge on the Red River, became among the most hated targets in North Vietnam, defying all attempts to close them permanently using conventional iron bombs. Many methods of attack were tried, to no avail.

Among the weapons found to be less than successful against bridges was the Martin Bullpup air-to-ground missile. Pilots had the unsettling experience of seeing these big white missiles actually bounce off well-constructed bridge spans. Bombs were not always reliable, there being instances of body and fin separation as well as malfunction in aircraft systems that could lead to a pilot unwittingly dropping not only his ordnance load, but the bomb racks as well.

Tactically, some missions were badly planned. Aircraft were sometimes loaded with the wrong ordnance to do the job, and sometimes it took time to determine which was the best course. Unfortunately, this often led to losses of pilots and aircraft.

On the plus side, Thunderchief in-commission rates remained high considering the number of hours flown, although the aircraft itself suffered from a number of shortcomings that were revealed only under the stress of combat. Among these was the fact that the F-105D did not have adequate protection in the rear fuselage.

If the F-105D was hit in the area just forward of the horizontal stabilator, the primary flight controls could be irreparably damaged due to the fact that the primary and backup hydraulic lines ran close together. Even a superficial hit from small-arms fire could take out two of the three systems. If that happened, the stabilator actuator locked in the up position, rendering the horizontal tail surfaces immovable and driving the aircraft's nose down, leaving the pilot with no option but to eject.

A temporary fix was made whereby the pilot could actuate a tailplane lock before all hydraulic fuel bled away, and Republic eventually cured the problem by rerouting the fluid lines to a less vulnerable location. Cooling of the aft fuselage also occupied the manufacturer's in-theater liaison personnel and the Air Force RAM—rapid area maintenance—teams who first went to SE Asia in 1965. While RAM specialists could deal with battle damage, the cooling problem demanded input from Republic's engineers back home in Farmingdale. Pilots found that the high engine temperatures generated by F-105s that were obliged to spend considerable periods of time in afterburner tended to impose an unacceptable fire risk. The Pratt and Whitney J75 was a tough power plant, and stories were legion as to its reliability under fire. But there were limits. . . . The problem was cured by introducing air intakes on each fuselage side to force cooling air into the aft engine compartment.

Rolling Thunder had hardly gotten underway when the US president imposed the first of a series of bombing halts, on 12 May. Designed to assess the results achieved thus far, and to show Hanoi that the US was eager to stop hostilities against North Vietnam the minute any moves toward peace were received, these pauses served only to give the enemy a little time to repair damage and consolidate its defenses. Worse, they broke the continuity of combat operations and confused and annoyed the pilots bent on getting on with the job at hand. Many wanted to complete their one hundred missions and become eligible for rotation home.

The first bombing halt lasted only until 18 May, the Joint Chiefs' analysis via CINCPAC showing that there had been little or no slowdown in guerrilla and Vietcong activity south of the 17th parallel. Supplies continued to feed through Laos from the ample stockpiles shipped into the North from its primary seaport, Haiphong. Still no directive to hit these worthwhile targets was forthcoming, and when strikes resumed, the same restrictions were in force.

Enemy defenses continued to take a toll of US aircraft,

and much thought was given to how best to equip a rescue force to get downed pilots out of North Vietnam before they could be captured. Many areas of dense jungle were thinly populated, and pilots forced to eject from crippled aircraft could be in limbo for hours or even days before the enemy reached their position. It was the US intention that that time period would be used to get rescue helicopters in.

It did, of course, happen that a man was captured almost immediately or that rescue forces were unable to get to the scene in time. A shoot-down was highly visible from the ground, and the Vietnamese made every effort to capture US pilots, so every rescue was a race against time. Initially, USAF in-theater rescue services were modest, being based around the short-ranged Kaman HH-43 Huskie, but in 1965 the first HH-3E Jolly Green Giant helos were based in Thailand at Nakhon Phanom. These machines became a lifeline to downed pilots, and some rescues, covered by Douglas A-1 Skyraiders with their awesome firepower, could be preluded by an amazing display of pyrotechnics if the enemy was too close to the pilot's position. The Jolly Greens and ''Sandy'' (the call sign of the Skyraiders) soon joined the ever-growing list of acronyms of the war, most of which saved vital time in radio transmissions.

On numerous occasions during the Rolling Thunder campaign, pilots flying battle-damaged Thuds were ''saved'' by refueling from KC-135 aerial tankers that were always on station during missions. So heavily laden was each F-105 that it would have been extremely difficult for the Air Force to maintain the pressure without a tanker force. After takeoff, the Thuds would invariably top off their tanks, fly the mission, and, depending on what maneuvering there had been in the target area in order to avoid the defenses, take on more fuel during target egress. If the fuel tanks had been damaged, a pilot could nurse his aircraft home almost by formating on a tanker and continually topping off—faster, it was hoped, than his fuel leaked completely away.

By the end of December 1965, the USAF had three squadrons of F-105s at Takhli and two at Korat, a total of ninety-four aircraft. The two Korat squadrons, the 421st and 469th, would become part of the 388th Tactical Fighter Wing on formation at that base in April 1966. Rotation of squadrons between the Thailand-based wings and those that remained outside the war zone would continue to spread combat experience as far as possible throughout TAC. Each Thai base also housed support units tasked with various duties, from providing tankers to developing and testing new tactics and weapons. One of the most important of these latter had already moved into Korat.

On 25 November 1965, the highly secret Wild Weasel Detachment of the 6234th TFW touched down, having left Eglin AFB on 21 November. A three-day weather-enforced layover in Hawaii had been spent on some unexpected R & R before the detachment could get under way for Thailand. Small in number and modest in equipment, constituted of but five less-than-new F-100F Super Sabres, this unit was the forerunner (it was identified as Wild Weasel I) of one of the most significant military formations to operate in the Vietnam War and one that had far-reaching implications in the time-honored battle of aerial strike forces versus ground defenses.

On 1 December, the F-100s flew the first Iron Hand sorties of the war. From then on, this code name would identify the Wild Weasel mission—the seeking out and destruction of North Vietnamese radars, principally the Fan Song SAM and Fire Can AAA guidance sets. Sustaining its first loss on 20 December, the Weasel detachment got better luck two days later, when the first radar "kill" was logged during a strike on the Yen Bai rail yards. The exposed Fan Song was duly dispatched with rocket fire.

A second bombing pause was announced on 24 December, heralding a massive US effort to gain a peace initiative with North Vietnam. The truce was in force until February 1966, again with no obvious reaction from Hanoi. When the strikes resumed, pilots found that the defenses were more intense than ever, but the existence of the Wild Weasels offered some welcome protection. Fighter pilots were often successful in evading SAMs, but slower, less agile aircraft were easy meat. This was demonstrated on 25 February, when an RB-66C of the 41st Tactical Reconnaissance Squadron, flying a mission to plot and jam Fan Song radar frequencies, was shot down. It was the second loss of one of these expensively modified Destroyers, and one that was widely felt.

But the need to seek out and destroy the SAM and AAA guidance radars was paramount if these serious threats to US aircraft were to be blunted, and research into developing a more effective carrier aircraft than the F-100F and improved, specialized weapons was already well advanced. Figures for the year 1965 had revealed that in 194 SAM firings, eleven US aircraft had been destroyed, a success rate of 5.7 percent. ECM pods cai-ried by the fighter bombers helped to keep the tally of kills directly attributable to SAMs within reasonable limits, pending the arrival of a dedicated Weasel platform armed with antiradiation missiles that could home directly onto Fan Song radar transmissions. In the meantime, TAC squadrons adopted close-formation radar-jamming flights. Although dangerous because these four-ship formations were vulnerable to both ground fire and MiG interception, they were effective.

It was found that each aircraft had to fly 1,500 feet behind the next one, and with 1,500- and 500-foot horizontal and vertical separation respectively, to maintain a good pod "tone." The next quartet followed 5,000 feet behind, with successive flights of eight 5,000 feet to the left of the leading formation.

If the antiradar formations could penetrate hostile territory without having to split up, they caused the SAM batteries no end of trouble: missiles went ballistic or they missed their intended targets by miles. In fact, throughout the war missile firings were out of all proportion to the number of aircraft they brought down. That is not to say that American pilots did not develop a healthy respect for them. It was, to say the least, unnerving to have a thirty-five-foot-long flaming telephone pole come shooting up through the overcast, turn ominously, and give chase. There were numerous reports of pilots throwing their aircraft all over the sky to shake off the deadly SA-2. It could be done, but it was a sweat-soaked, exhausting period laced with sheer terror while the chase lasted.

On 1 April 1966, a new Air Force command was created, with its headquarters at Saigon's Tan Son Nhut airport, as part of an attempt to streamline the previously

tortuous command structure that ran operations in South
Vietnam and Thailand. Seventh Air Force replaced the
2nd Air Division and broke away from the jurisdiction
of the 13th Air Force in the Philippines. Seventh reported
directly to CINCPAC in Hawaii. It was by no means a
perfect arrangement, but it was an improvement.

The primary problem was that no individual or office
had control of all the air assets the US had at its disposal.
With four separate services—five counting the South
Vietnamese air force—supporting combat aircraft or helicopters, and organizations such as Strategic Air Command refusing to delegate mission planning to another
command, considerable time was taken to inform all
"interested parties." In this delay between detection of
targets by reconnaissance to an attack being made, the
field situation could change completely. This was particularly true of ground support in the South, although
the Thailand-based Wings also were affected by the requirement to disseminate target information to one and
all, up to and including the secretary of defense, prior to
an air strike. In the view of many, it was a system that
handed nearly all the initiatives to the enemy.

A week after the formation of Seventh Air Force, the
388th TFW was organized at Korat. The Wing had been
activated on 14 March under its ninth commander, Colonel Monroe S. Sams, at Korat, where it replaced the
provisional 6234th TFW. On 8 April, the Wing took over
control of the 421st and 469th Squadrons, these being
joined by three more, the 44th (on 25 April) and the 13th
and 34th (on 15 May). In addition, there was the Weasel
detachment, which would remain at Korat more or less
for the duration of hostilities

Of these units, the two high-numbered squadrons were the most experienced, both of them having flown combat from Korat since late 1965. In reality, although the Wing number changed, it was very much business as usual, although there developed a healthy rivalry between the 355th Wing at Takhli and the denizens of Korat. As the war progressed, squadrons rotated into both wings at different periods, and for some two years they flew the same aircraft. Operational procedures followed by each Wing did, however, differ quite significantly.

The 388th came into being at a time when a bomb shortage was felt by many of the units in Southeast Asia. Denied officially, it was nevertheless true that strikes were sent off with reduced loads—not fewer aircraft. It would have been logical to put the maximum load on a smaller number of aircraft, but such was the atmosphere of the time that logic often played a very small part in what went on. Some elements were seemingly obsessed with a thing they called "sortie rate," and consequently the pilots went out in Thuds loaded not with the full 10,000 lb of bombs, but half that weight, or less.

A depletion of ordnance stocks, unforeseen in the early days of the "short war," was soon rectified, but some pretty succinct comments were made about it at the time. It was true enough that the tonnage of bombs dropped since the start of Rolling Thunder had been little short of staggering; nobody could possibly have estimated just how much high explosive it would take to subdue North Vietnam—and in early 1966, this was still a totally unknown factor. Hanoi was making no peace overtures, and militarily the country was still very strong.

With a nominal strength of 144 Thunderchiefs, the

seven TAC squadrons in Thailand maintained the pressure on the North, hitting a long list of targets, many of which did not seem to warrant the weight of bombs aimed at them—and certainly not the lives of the highly trained men who had been led to expect anything but the kind of war rules they were fighting under. Invariably, anything that was useful to the North Vietnamese war effort and the sustaining of the civilian population was heavily defended, and the Thud attrition rate spiraled accordingly. To their lasting credit, these men got on with the job they had been given to do, damning the critics and the statisticians who worked out that it was all but impossible for a Thud driver to complete his mandatory one hundred missions before being rotated home.

But any man who did complete the course—and there were plenty—found that the mid-1960s Air Force that wasn't in combat was, if anything, even more difficult to hack than the crazy war operating out of Thailand. The rules of the game there might have been weird and the weather conditions lousy, but the camaraderie was of a very high order indeed. More than a few went back and flew a second tour.

Intelligence reports of the air-to-air opposition to US air strikes noted that the number of MiGs encountered was never very large and that the buildup of the North Vietnamese Air Force was slow. Until the spring of 1966, the main interceptor type flown by the opposition was the MiG-17. While highly maneuverable and well armed, it was technically a generation behind modern US fighters. But on 23 April, there came the disturbing news that the North had some MiG-21s available for combat.

Reckoned to be less of a sign that the small NVAF

had rapidly come of age than a desire on the part of the
Russians to find out how well one of their best fighters
did in actual combat with the Americans, the appearance
of the MiG-21 could have been an indicator of wholesale
NVAF reequipment, although the modest size of the force
did not make this very likely. In any event, the MiG-21
was undoubtedly a new factor to take into account. Even
a small number of them, if well deployed, could present
a serious challenge, particularly as, unlike the MiG-17,
they were AAM-capable.

A short time after the initial pilot reports of the MiG-
21, the first one was destroyed by a Phantom, which
brought the threat more into perspective. Destruction of
the newer MiG version was to be reserved for the Phantom throughout the war, although the two Thud wings
gave a good account of themselves against the MiG-17.
In the last phase of the air war, the 388th would itself
figure in the list of MiG-21 kills, when it was partially
equipped with the F-4E, the Phantom that introduced the
much-in-demand built-in gun.

Much the same type of gun, the General Electric
M-61, had been fitted to the F-105 from the start of
production, and pilots in combat often found it a useful
supplement to standard, expendable ordnance against
ground targets. When it came to air-to-air combat, although the F-105D was cleared to fire a single Sidewinder
from one wing station on each side, there were only three
recorded instances of Thuds destroying MiG-17s with
AIM-9s, and one of these was a combined missile and
gun kill. Gunfire did the job on the rest of the enemy
aircraft downed by F-105s during the course of the war.

As for freefall ordnance, by far the most frequently

used munition was the 750-lb general-purpose bomb. Streamlined for improved aerodynamic properties, the "slicks" packed a punch well able to destroy rigid structures. The F-105D was able to carry a maximum of sixteen 750-pounders, utilizing the four-wing hardpoints and the multiple ejector rack under the fuselage center section. A bomb load used only on short-range missions, this gave way to the more typical load of six bombs on the centerline rack, and two drop tanks and one more bomb on each outer wing pylon. Heavier bombs were carried on occasion, as were blunt-nosed cluster bombs, and the wing pylons were often occupied by missiles or ECM pods, as the nature of the threat changed.

3

WITH two Thud Wings in place in Thailand, the United States had a more organized tactical strike force that was able to attack any target in North Vietnam. The target list was continually scrutinized, but many people were of the opinion that even by the spring of 1966, the enemy had been allowed to grow too strong, particularly in fixed gun defenses. The target restrictions were felt to be arbitrary at best; at worst, they were seen to favor the enemy rather than friendly aircraft. Pilots took the ban on what to them seemed to be priority targets as a personal slur on their ability to bomb accurately, and the meddling of high command from their remote headquarters was irksome.

It is on record that this scrutiny of the war over the North sometimes entered the realm of comic relief. For example, Thud pilots will long retell the story of one of their number who was poised for takeoff for another mission in harm's way, only to be recalled from the cockpit by a telephone call. On the other end was none other than Secretary McNamara, who wanted to know what ordnance the pilot was about to haul across the 17th parallel. Told that the load for that day was napalm, McNamara said no. Wondering how someone in Washington could interpret more about the target from photos and maps than he could, the pilot nevertheless took off with a different load.

"Saber" Sams did not hold the reins of the 388th for long. He handed control over to Brigadier General William S. Chairsell on 17 August 1966. By that time, the 388th was able to celebrate the first confirmed MiG kill by an F-105, on 29 June. The victor was Major Fred Tracy, flying as number two in a four-ship Iron Hand SAM suppression flight.

Coming off target, the flight encountered four MiG-17s some twenty-five miles north-northwest of Hanoi. Aircraft numbers three and four in the American formation broke and dived as the MiGs fired. Leaving these two, the MiGs concentrated on Tracy and the leader, although only two enemy aircraft actually engaged, the second pair apparently covering the attackers.

Putting their aircraft into afterburner, the two Thud pilots continued a diving left turn and jettisoned their ordnance. The lead MiG opened up and hit Tracy's aircraft. By pure chance one of the 23mm shells knocked his hand off the throttle, promptly taking it out of 'burner. The MiG's fire also damaged some instruments, the gunsight, and oxygen equipment.

But the MiG pilot misjudged his closing speed and overshot Tracy. He momentarily hung there in Tracy's twelve o'clock before he began taking 20mm rounds. Tracy fired two hundred rounds and observed about ten hits. The MiG rolled over and did a split-S into cloud.

Still in the fight, the second MiG-17 had meanwhile hit the lead Thud, the pilot of which fired with no visible result. MiG number four was hosed by the fourth Thud, but again without hits being observed, and the action terminated, Tracy having already left to nurse his damaged machine home, covered by number three in the flight. He made it, and there was due cause for celebration when the news of his success was made known at Korat.

A MiG kill by a Thud driver was then still something of a rarity, and the young Turks who flew up north felt, as fighter pilots, that it was really something to celebrate. Saber Sams thought otherwise. Before he departed Korat, he admonished his eager pilots not to perform victory rolls over the base. He was quite adamant on the point, as many commanders before him had been. Naturally, such a ban did not go down well with the pilots, and succeeding Wing commanders were more lenient.

A MiG kill was something the 388th sorely needed to get a little publicity. It seemed that most of what got into print about the Thud Wings in Thailand was about the 355th at Takhli, and although this sort of favoritism was not intended, it rankled, particularly with the pilots. They were taking the same risks, so where were the news people to tell their stories?

Neither of the Thai bases had at first been the epitome of a modern air base, and Korat was marginally more remote, hot, and dusty than Takhli. A building program was necessary at both when the USAF moved in, and making them hospitable took time. Add to this the fact

that the bombing of North Vietnam was not an action
that the US or Thailand particularly wanted to publicize
in the early 1960s, it was small wonder that those who
served in Thailand felt they had been forgotten. Then
again, military men do not always appreciate someone
with a camera and notebook looking over their shoulder,
and the 388th decided that there was something to be
said for being left to get on with a tough job, one that
had generated a good deal of unwelcome publicity outside. There was little choice but to accept the situation
with alacrity. Eventually, the 388th took to calling itself
the Avis Wing, after the well-known car-rental adver-
tisements of the time. The implied assurance that ''we
try harder (even if we're number two)'' gave some satisfaction to the troops at Korat.

It was said that one of the reasons the press always
seemed to visit Takhli and not Korat was that the 355th's
squadrons tended to enjoy a more individualistic approach to mission planning and execution. While there
were many Takhli pilots who swore by the low-level
approach to beating the guns, MiGs, and SAMs, the
388th often flew RB-66-directed Skyspot missions utilizing big formations at medium (10,000 to 15,000 feet)
altitudes, where they were more vulnerable to ground
fire.

On the positive side, a large formation of F-105s dropping together on a target represented a considerable
weight of bombs, and it should be remembered that there
were many ''bomber men'' running the air war. Their
predilection for sending Thuds in like the high-level
bombers of a past era could hardly be ignored, despite

the risks. In the final analysis, the pilots did what they were ordered to do and tried their best to minimize the risks.

It was very much a case of read the frag, shrug the shoulders, and fly the mission. Pilots had enough problems of their own on every sortie North. There was little time available to dwell on why they were doing the job in a particular way.

Korat in fact became an impressive base, one that is still used today by US fighters, although controlled by the Thai Air Force. The 9,000-foot paved runway was enough to safely get the heavily laden 388th Thunderchiefs into the air, and every one had its own concrete hardstanding. The living accommodations and administrative area spread into the surrounding countryside, and it rapidly took on the air of a home away from home, as does most every other US air base throughout the world.

Willy Chairsell's tenure at the head of the 388th included some of the toughest missions the Wing was to undertake. A commander who didn't fly himself, Chairsell nevertheless backed his people against the dictates from above and helped the Wing make its mark. Like other TAC officers in charge of an operational combat outfit in Southeast Asia, Chairsell was glad to keep the top brass at arm's length.

By the summer of 1966, the target list was still growing to include those that had previously remained off limits. The 388th was awarded its first Air Force Outstanding Unit Award in June 1966, for carrying out heavy attacks on the Hanoi oil-storage area on the 29th and 30th of that month. POL—petrol, oil and lubricants—were ob-

vious targets for air strikes, particularly if North Vietnam's centers for these important resources could be
eliminated.

There is little doubt that the Hanoi oil facility was very
badly damaged (a subsequent USAF release estimated
loss of production and stocks to be as high as ninety-five
percent by the successful Air Force strike). Only one
Thud was lost, and on the following day a Navy Skyhawk
attack was even better: no aircraft went down to ground
fire. The resulting quick and efficient dispersal of oil
supplies by the enemy meant that POL targets would
henceforth figure regularly in the target list for both the
Thailand-based Air Force Wings and the Navy carrier
force. As before, it was widely believed that attacks on
a target vital to the North's war potential had come too
late.

It immediately became obvious just how much the oil
strikes got Hanoi's attention. The main, thirty-two-tank
farm hit in the July raids was situated only four miles
from the city center. Loud protests were rapidly forthcoming. The US "air pirates" seemed at last to be achieving some results. Strangely, instead of taking satisfaction
from this reaction, the US government promptly made
any target within ten miles of Hanoi off limits to airmen.

Dispersion of gasoline and oil supplies into the countryside made for increasingly difficult targets; it meant
in effect that every truck, every railroad flatcar, and every
barge could be moving lubricants in containers as small
as fifty-five-gallon drums. Also, an overoptimistic or
faulty piece of intelligence fed into the tactical air system
could and did lead to an incredibly high wastage of munitions on targets such as innocent-looking hootches. In

reality, these flimsy structures were often as worthless as they appeared to be. North Vietnam was, however, an armed camp unlike any warring nation before it. The wily enemy was quite capable of stashing fuel in peaceful villages knowing full well that the inhabitants could all be wiped out in an air strike. The same cynicism was evident in the placing of AAA in areas full of civilian dwellings.

The US had little choice but to plaster every suspect structure. When a hidden fuel store was ignited in a bombing or strafing run, the resulting explosions showed that there was some merit in the hunt. It was when men got killed or wounded and aircraft shot down or damaged that the economics of the thing simply did not stack up.

Washington was beginning to see that its bombing policy against the North was simply not working. So, from this point on, the smaller targets were increasingly interspersed with ones that did seem to achieve lasting damage. Throughout the remainder of 1966, the Rolling Thunder target list expanded in Route Packs V and VI —the only areas that really counted.

On 9 July, the 388th and 355th were dispatched against the North's rail network. The yards at Thanh Hoa, Phu Ly, Ninh Binh, and Vinh were blasted. Rail interdiction was assigned to the Air Force, and thousands of tons of supplies were destroyed both by bombing and strafing. MiG bases remained immune, although the increasing number of Phantoms on hand to fly combat air patrols with F-105 strike forces kept this particular hazard within acceptable limits.

From the end of the monsoon season in late April until June, eight MiGs were lost in a round of air encounters

in which the NVAF was notably more aggressive.
Against pilots equally keen to engage, the Vietnamese
pilots were more or less forced to tighten their tactics:
no longer could they execute hit-and-run passes on Thunderchief formations protected by F-4s, as the superior
performance of the Phantom rapidly put the MiGs at a
disadvantage.

There had been more than one month's break in confirmed MiG kills before Major Kenneth T. Blank knocked
down another for the 388th on 18 August. Major Blank,
of the 34th TFS, intercepted two MiG-17s that were after
an Iron Hand flight of SAM suppressors. Blank, call sign
Honda 02, fired at a MiG that in turn had the lead Iron
Hand Thud in its sights.

Intent on his victim, the MiG pilot failed to watch his
six o'clock, where Blank's big, hungry Thud was snapping at his heels. Some two hundred rounds left the barrel
of the major's M61 cannon at a range of 400 to 600 feet.
The MiG promptly burst into flames and went into an
inverted dive. The wingman fled. Watching the enemy
fighter hit the ground, Blank reflected that the entire
engagement had taken less than two minutes.

That a well-flown F-105 was more than a match for a
MiG-17 had been proven before; both the Korat and
Takhli Wings were able to emphasize the fact on 21
September. Two MiGs fell to the 20mm gunfire of First
Lieutenant Karl W. Richter of the 388th and the 355th's
Fred Wilson.

Among the missions fragged for that day was a covering flight (call sign Ford) of three F-105Ds for an Iron
Hand F-105F flight supporting a large strike force attacking the Dap Cau highway and railroad bridge. Rich-

ter, flying in the number-three slot, with his wingman as number four, turned into the MiGs as they closed in on the US formation. After failing to catch the other two Thuds, which had been their intended targets, the enemy pilots went into a left turn. Richter closed to within 2,000 feet and fired. He hit the first MiG-17 and the other broke sharply.

Richter's wingman, Ford 04, fired at this enemy fighter but missed. Richter got in position to fire again at his original opponent, and this time the result of the burst of gunfire was spectacular. The youngest pilot to score a MiG kill in Vietnam, twenty-three-year-old Richter reported:

"I saw my twenty-millimeter rounds start to sparkle on his right wing the second time I fired. His right wing fell off. As I flew past I saw the MiG's canopy pop off."

Little doubt about that one. The enemy pilot ejected safely, and both Richter and his wingman followed the stricken MiG's flight into the ground. The Air Force duly marked the double MiG kill by the pair of Thud pilots on the same day—definitely cause to crack a few warm beers.

By the date of the 388th's third MiG kill, Willy Chairsell had left the Wing and handed over the leadership to Colonel Edward B. Burdett, who was to lead it until 17 November 1966. Before he vacated the hot seat, the Thailand-based Thud Wings were into another round of intensive air operations.

4

THE last quarter of 1966 through January 1967 was a period marked by unusually intense MiG activity. The North Vietnamese pilots challenged their US opposite numbers on all but four days when strike operations were flown. Despite the protection they now had, the Thud Wings were still vulnerable to interception, and from September to December, sorties to targets located in Route Packs IV, V, and VI resulted in 107 aircraft (55.73 percent of the 192 actually engaged by MiGs) being forced to jettison their loads.

Such figures were annoying, particularly to the sortie-rate statisticians, obsessed as they were with tons of bombs on a given target on such and such a day. More seriously, pilots who were forced to drop prematurely relied heavily on their colleagues to annihilate the target with fewer bombs. If not, they'd all be back on the roster another day.

Young, tough, and somewhat irreverent over the war they were fighting, Thud pilots began painting slogans, cartoons, and names on their aircraft, just as men in previous wars had done. This might have surprised some people, and it didn't always sit well with members of the brass. The Thud's sixty-five-foot fuselage was an ideal canvas for what has come to be known as "nose art," and in any other war, large cartoons and names might have suddenly appeared. But even in this respect, Southeast Asia was unique. Anyone desiring to give an F-105 a little personality had to be far more subtle lest some ground-bound weeny went running to authority to report that the flyers were defacing government property.

Consequently, what appeared was not nose art in the accepted sense but more "under-the-wing" art. The names and drawings could thus be literally kept in the shade, hidden from all but the most inquisitive eyes. Someone (whose name was apparently not recorded) also devised a scheme whereby an aircraft name was applied in stylish silver gothic script on a dark background along the outer face of the forward-jutting air intakes. Many Thuds began to sport these identifiers, and along with small areas of color trim and some application of squadron and wing badges, the otherwise anonymous airplanes reflected a growing esprit de corps, despite the restrictions.

As 1966 drew to a close, it was fairly obvious that the USAF was destined to retain a presence in Thailand. The war showed no sign of running down; in fact, the opposite was true. On 12 September, a massive five-hundred-sortie assault was launched on supply areas, transportation, SAM sites, and coastal traffic—the heaviest series of air strikes to date.

"Flak so thick you could walk on it" was a phase coined by bomber crews in World War II to denote a particularly tough mission. It was grimly relevant over North Vietnam on nearly every raid. So concentrated had the enemy defenses become that it was by no means unusual for Thud drivers to lose sight of their wingmen in the dense smoke of exploding AAA shells. Diving into that maelstrom of exploding steel looked like certain suicide, yet pilots did it day after day, week after week. Sometimes their aircraft took hits, but often they came home unscathed. It was often like trying to dodge raindrops in a cloudburst.

Still, the losses were heavy, considering the size of the TAC F-105 force based in Thailand, and the fact was that when the Republic production lines closed in 1964, the only replacement for a downed Thud was one that had been patched up or come in from another theater. A new Thud was now a thing of the past.

Figures put out at the end of 1966 gave the stark fact that 126 F-105s had been lost to combat or to combat-related causes. It was small wonder that men who were there reckoned that flying a Thud over North Vietnam was the most dangerous job in the world.

For every debit figure there should be a credit balance. In this case, it was that for all their grievous losses over the North, the 388th and 355th Wings hauled a grand total of 165,000 tons of bombs and other munitions across the 17th parallel and in so doing flew 106,500 sorties during the year. Even this did not result in any waving of the white flag from Hanoi, and in the South, the Americans and their allies were still fighting hard.

Militarily, if the scale of enemy action in the South was any yardstick, all the air effort against the North did not appear to be achieving a great deal. But in fact, the American bombing was having a very great effect, both physically and psychologically. The enemy needed to be increasingly sustained by assistance from outside, and even basic survival was becoming a daily problem, culminating in the large-scale evacuation of Hanoi the following year.

But nobody who flew "downtown," as the pilots dubbed a flight into the higher route packs of North Vietnam, could deny that the enemy was getting stronger and more aggressive. On 2 December 1966, a date thereafter known as Black Friday, the US air forces lost no less than eight aircraft.

On 14 December 1966, the USAF was on the receiving end of an AA-2 Atoll missile fired by a MiG-21. An NVAF pilot nailed an F-105D with the weapon, which closely resembled the US Sidewinder AAM. It was another escalation in the air war, which seemed no nearer a conclusion than it had twelve months before. As the year closed, Johnson instigated the first of two short breaks in combat operations, marking Christmas and New Year's Day.

On 2 January 1967, with the short bombing halt still in effect, a massive force totaling 96 aircraft was launched from various bases in Thailand. It included tankers, EB-66s, and RC-121 radar surveillance planes. But the main purpose of the operation was to bring the Vietnamese MiGs up to intercept. Once they were up, it was hoped, the enemy 'scope watchers would see a large US strike force and vector the fighters accordingly. Then the American trap would be sprung. The NVAF would find not heavily laden Thuds but armed-to-the-teeth F-4 Phantoms of Robin Olds's crack 8th TFW. Then the US pilots would take the chance to avenge Black Friday.

Spearheading the Operation Bolo force were Wild Weasel EF-105s from Korat, escorted by F-104 Starfighters drawn from the 435th TFS at Nakhon Phanom. On this occasion, the escort was not needed. The ruse worked, and at the end of the day, the North Vietnamese Air Force was the poorer by seven expensive MiG-21s.

As delighted as the F-4 pilots were at this chance to hit the enemy hard, higher echelons questioned the huge cost of sending ninety-six aircraft out in order to knock down seven of the enemy. By that yardstick, it was indeed a small return—but one that every pilot in Thailand welcomed as a substitute for bombing the enemy air force on its airfields. For a few more months, these were to remain on the restricted list, to the consternation of every man who flew North.

Washington was, however, closely scrutinizing the target list, and Rolling Thunder kept widening in scope as the United States grew increasingly frustrated at the nonreaction from Hanoi. Americans were voicing their disapproval, although an equally strong voice supported the US presence in Southeast Asia. For some time, the for and against factions were about equal in number. The war, apart from another break for the Vietnamese Tet New Year vacation from 8 to 12 February, ground on.

The most recent halt made five, counting the two short ones of late 1966 and early 1967. None of them had achieved a thing. A stand-down in operations benefited some people, though: the TAC ground crews on the Thai bases welcomed the chance to slow the pace. During the intensive strike periods, there was rarely any such thing as day or night for the ground crews. Hot days gave way to slightly cooler nights, and the hours of darkness were preferred for some duties. But at least there was little likelihood that a new offensive would bring the air bases in range of enemy mortar fire, as had happened in South Vietnam.

By the spring of 1967, there were signs that US patience was running out: the targets were getting nearer and nearer to the "forbidden circle" surrounding Hanoi and Haiphong. In March, the F-105s and F-4s were briefed to attack one of the few worthwhile targets in the North, namely the Thai Nguyen steel works, thirty-five miles north of the capital. On the same day, the fighter bombers were over the Canal des Rapides, only four miles from Hanoi.

The raid on the steel works was pressed home through intense AAA fire. As had happened before, the planners then sat back to analyze the poststrike photos. And waited. Another attack was scheduled for the 29th, and thereafter the steel works appeared on the target list continually. Time was wasted in trying to put it completely out of action with small-scale strikes.

For the pilots giving their all in the unequal struggle with the world's toughest air defense net, April 1967 was the most notable month of the war. On the 24th of that month, they were briefed to bomb North Vietnam's principal airfields. A large-scale air effort was launched, just in case the powers that be changed their collective minds again. Both Thud wings participated, and bombs rained down on the hardstandings and runways at Kep, Hoa Lac, and Kien An. As if to prove that this was exactly the way to blunt an enemy air force, the strikes destroyed 20 MiGs. Previously, it would have taken months of hard fighting to shoot down that number in aerial combat. As it was, there were fifty engagements with MiGs that month.

May saw the USAF and Navy going all out with an expanded target list to finally wrap up this crazy war. The bombers were back over Kep and Hoc Lac on the 2nd, and rail and transportation targets were hit hard. To take the edge off these penetrations, the MiGs rose to do battle with the Americans on seventy-two occasions.

On one, 13 May, Major Maurice Seaver, Jr., (alias Kimona 02) of the 388th's 44th TFS, put paid to a MiG-17, one of seven to fall that day. Two kills were scored by F-4s, and no fewer than five were notched up by F-105s.

It was a busy day for the Korat and Takhli Thud Wings. Not all attacks were made in force, single flights of four aircraft or two or three flights often having more chance of foxing the defenses, getting in quickly, bombing, and getting out even faster. Using this technique, multiple small targets (as the majority were) could be struck at the same time and, it was hoped, divide the defenses, particularly enemy interceptors.

On the 13th, a flight of 388th Wing F-105Ds attacked the Vinh Yen army barracks, while the 355th Wing put two flights over the Vien Yen railroad yard. Pulling up after his bomb run, Major Seaver saw a camouflaged MiG-17 at his ten o'clock, about 1,000 feet away. Pulling

in behind the enemy fighter, Seaver opened fire. The
clock ticked off just ninety seconds. In that space of time,
Seaver's gunfire impacted the MiG and tore off one wing.
Only at the last second did it break right, but that might
have been the force of the explosion. Major Seaver was
of the opinion that the MiG driver had not even seen
him.

Thud kills with guns were sometimes envied by the
MiGCAP Phantom jocks, particularly after one or more
hairy engagements in which they had seen their missiles
disappear harmlessly into midair, fail to lock on to the
target, or to fire at all. It happened all too frequently,
and the F-4 community kept up its lobbying for the aircraft to have gun as well as missile capability—a requirement that was about to be fulfilled.

That the rules of engagement were tough to follow at
times was shown in a Department of Defense report issued on 15 May. The report admitted, guardedly, that
one Thud pilot had, during egress from one of the raids
on Kep, gone down over China. The release did not say
where the pilot had flown from or his ultimate fate.

The fate that did await American pilots who fell into
North Vietnamese hands was already widely known outside the military community. Many were tortured, and
all suffered deprivations that made a mockery of the terms
of the Geneva Convention. Americans at home were
shocked to see and hear on TV newscasts their men
admitting their guilt as terror fliers. A few probably
guessed correctly that the confessions had been made
under extreme duress. Worse news came only much later:
a number of pilots in captivity had paid with their lives
for a cause that was, to many, lost before it even began.

Early in June, the air at Korat rang to jubilant accolades of more MiG kills for the old "Ultra Hog," the "Lead Sled" of yesteryear that had caused such concern in TAC planning circles when the fate of America—if the worst happened—was vested in a few Wings of interceptors. How the F-105 would have fared on such missions against enemy bombers is academic: Vietnam was now the front line. And lacking the political will to use the "big stick" to beat the enemy quickly, the US sent tactical fighter bombers on hundreds of thousands of dangerous sorties against factories and other hard targets while down south SAC's B-52s systematically annihilated enemy trees and grass. It was small wonder that those men who completed their hundred missions into the northern route packs were hooked as surely as a drug addict; hooked not on self-destruction but by the sheer adrenaline rush of evading destruction by others and the tight-knit comradeship of their peers who did the same job and overcame the same dangers. Mostly, these men were as blood brothers who rode the very pinnacle of their trade. The higher the odds, the harder the fraternity of danger was cemented.

By tradition, fighter pilots who fly hard like to play hard. But for the Wings based in Thailand in the 1960s, the chance for the usual R & R activities was limited, at least locally. A few days' leave would bring on the lure of Bangkok, where the shops, restaurants, and fleshpots welcomed US dollars with ever-open arms. But for the men whose daily round was to fly into North Vietnam, the risk of overindulgence were sharpened by the fact that if the worst happened, room service at the Hanoi Hilton did not include drugs like penicillin to take care of social diseases. That sobering thought made the base bar facilities a little more attractive than usual.

The continual watch and subsequent pounding of lines of enemy communication were an integral part of Rolling Thunder. The two rail lines linking North Vietnam with China were particularly heavily interdicted so that major breaks made previously were not repaired or bypassed and that rolling stock and locomotives were permanently denied the enemy. Bac Giang had a combined rail/highway bridge on the northeast line that led to Nanning over the Chinese border. Each major rail section was given a code number, the northeast one identified as "RR 2." It was, like all such locations in the North, a magnet for US bombs and had been attacked on many occasions before. On 3 June 1967, the 388th went back to Bac Giang.

With the bombers releasing their loads on the bridge and adjacent rail yards, the strike was carried out successfully. Iron Hand flights integrated with the strike flights, their pilots maintaining the necessary formation to enable the ECM pods to do their work against the SA-2 and AAA radars. Leading one of the strike/Iron Hand elements that day were Captain Larry Wiggins and Major Ralph Kuster, Jr., of Hambone Flight.

During the run-in to the target and about fifteen miles out from the point where the bombers rolled in to start their runs, heavy 85- and 100mm AAA opened up.

In order to even up the odds a little, part of the attack force would be prebriefed to go after the guns, usually by dive bombing them. This type of attack had the dual advantage of knocking out some guns and identifying others in the area on gun-camera film. Those AAA sites would be noted and alerted to crews making subsequent strikes. A short burst of the M-61 exposed the film, and it was this task that Kuster completed while the railroad strike proceeded.

As Kuster recovered, he was about 1,500 feet behind the flight lead. Wiggins was then about a mile behind. About six miles off the target, the lead called in three MiG-17s at ten o'clock low, range two miles. Lead and second and third F-105s in the flight started a hard left turn, but number four became separated. He also began to turn but found the second Thud flight off the target a little close for comfort. He narrowly avoided a collision. Number four elected to stay with this flight during the withdrawal.

Meanwhile, the three MiGs had gone into a tight left-hand orbit at about 5,000 feet altitude, and initial maneuvers failed to offer any firing chances. Both the Thuds and MiG-17s had completed one and a half circles before Wiggins saw his chance.

Wiggins's AIM-9B was aimed at the third MiG, which attempted to evade the missile. The pilot almost made it. The Sidewinder exploded alongside the MiG's tailpipe, causing the aircraft to trail white smoke. Wiggins closed as the enemy fighter rolled over and began to go down. Making sure of his kill, the American pilot fired 376 rounds of 20mm. Despite Wiggins's high angle-off, the MiG exploded in flame and crashed.

While this action was taking place, the first MiG had closed with the Thud flight leader and had been joined by the second one in the original ''wheel.'' These fighters

were respectively a mile and half a mile off the lead.
Kuster called them in. Lead responded with "If you can
get one, go get him!"

Kuster did so. He was in a good position to nail the
lead MiG, leaving the second one to the F-105 flight
leader. Kuster got a forty-five-degree angle-off shot while
pulling 5 to 6 G. His lead was not enough, and the Thud
was unable to track the MiG-17 through the turn. Kuster
executed a high-speed yo-yo to reduce his overshoot, and
the MiG reversed into a hard right turn.

This action by the enemy pilot partially solved Kuster's
difficulty in tracking him, and after a few more maneuvers, he fired again, from 1,200 feet. Again no hits were
observed.

Kuster was obviously up against a MiG driver with
some experience, for the tussle went on. The MiG rolled
left, banked, and dived. Kuster closed at about two
hundred knots overtake speed, but his adversary anticipated the pass and went into a smooth, tight descending
left turn, seemingly reducing speed to force the F-105 to
overshoot again.

Kuster was not going to let this one go. Pulling maximum G, just short of pilot red-out, Kuster desperately
sought enough lead on the MiG so that it had to fly into
his cone of fire. One last trick was to flick-roll the Thud,
killing off speed, and place the gunsight pipper ahead of
the quarry. Kuster was very close, less than two hundred
feet away. It worked. The nose of the Thud snapped out
a stream of shells.

This time, there was no way that the MiG driver could
avoid. The shells tore into the underside of his left wing,
which promptly exploded inboard of the underslung ex-

ternal fuel tank. Kuster ducked the oncoming stream of debris aimed at his aircraft by twenty-five feet. He passed below the stricken MiG as it rolled inverted and crashed. All the way down it had remained inverted. It took only four to five seconds to impact, and no 'chute was observed.

Kuster's kill was the first for his squadron at that time, the 13th, while Wiggins's victory had made it two for the 469th TFS to date. Overall, the 388th Wing had destroyed seven MiG-17s since the start of Rolling Thunder operations.

5

WHILE the F-105 Wings in Thailand carried on their iron bomb war with increasing help from F-4 Phantom units, great efforts were being made to make air strikes on the North more effective. The best way to achieve this end was for all strike aircraft dispatched from Thai bases to reach the target and be as free as possible to make accurate bomb runs. This situation could only prevail if the missile and gun defenses were knocked out or their radar guidance nullified; gradually, the US worked toward this goal, which required an intensive effort on new weapons and, above all, electronic systems coupled to a better antiradiation missile.

During the summer of 1967, Navy A-6 Intruders became the first aircraft in inventory able to use the General Dynamics Standard ARM (antiradiation missile). Developed from a Navy surface-to-air missile, the Standard packed a hefty punch. It was fifteen feet long and weighed over 1,350 pounds. It was also faster than the Shrike ARM, with a maximum speed of around Mach 2.5 and an effective range of thirty-five miles. The Air Force began tests to mate Standard ARM to the F-105F during this period, with a view to having the missile fully operational in 1968.

In the meantime, the Wild Weasel war went on with "first generation" weaponry adapted for the new role of attacking radars and other passive defenses, equipment that was vital to an effective gun and missile "ring of steel" around the main targets. However, such was the flood of replacement parts, new units, and ammunition from China and the Soviet Union that reached North Vietnam through her principal seaport, Haiphong, that whatever the US did could only hamper the defense net on a local basis. On the other hand, if local air superiority could be achieved long enough for the target to be badly hit, North Vietnam would eventually have nothing worthwhile to defend. So went the theory, which was also extrapolated into the belief that once widespread destruction and disruption of essential supplies and industrial output had taken place, the North would have little choice but to cease its war in South Vietnam. But the war managers of the 1960s overlooked the fact that without ground operations to support the air effort, North Vietnam was unlikely ever to give up while she was supplied from outside.

By mid-1967, Rolling Thunder had caused widespread destruction, although many important targets remained intact under the ROE. Increasing US frustration from the Oval Office down caused constant scrutiny of target lists, most of which were more than adequately covered by aerial reconnaissance overflights. The Air Force alone took thousands of pre- and poststrike photos to show what had—and what had not—been achieved by the bombing campaign. A great many photographs indicated all too clearly that North Vietnam was still in business both as a light industrial and agricultural center and a collecting point for supplies from nations sympathetic to Ho Chi Minh's cause. Rail traffic was still running across the country's two main rail links with China, using the Paul Doumer and "Dragon's Jaw" bridges, industrial plants were still producing, and military and civilian personnel were still being fed.

Not yet able to hit the enemy's heartland, the Air Force strike wings in Thailand continued to gnaw away at his arteries, in tune to the whims of the Pentagon, which still sought an old-fashioned and, in this case, unrealistic victory—through force of arms. The war was starting to become a grueling, will- and mind-sapping slugging match, seemingly without end or, to some, purpose.

As time passed, the fighter pilots who took the war to North Vietnam grew in number. They felt that they had unwittingly built enclaves of the brave at Korat and Takhli and the other Thai and South Vietnamese bases, and, in the face of indifference and at times outright hostility from fellow Americans, they drew closer in the comradeship of combat. Any man who had penetrated the higher route packs of North Vietnam had a circle of friends who had done the same job. This camaraderie extended to other branches of the Air Force, such as tanker crews, recon pilots, and the men who flew rescue missions in helicopters and the tough old Spad, the venerable A-1 Skyraider. But it was the jet jockeys, the

Thunderchief and Phantom pilots and their back-seaters, who bore the brunt of the strike missions. These individuals had their counterparts in the Navy, where F-8 Crusader and Phantom men, not to mention Intruder and Skyhawk pilots, shared the same risks. But there was not often the chance to discuss tactics with the carrier pilots, whose operations were fundamentally different from those of the Air Force, even though the end result was designed to be much the same.

USAF fighter pilots attempted to create a pool of experience that could be shared by men coming into Thailand and who were new to the air war "in the barrel." By the second summer of Rolling Thunder, numerous pilots had left SE Asia for good, their tours complete. If these men did not share their invaluable experience with others, the job would have to be learned all over again. To meet that challenge, they formed the Red River Valley Fighter Pilots' Association in 1967. This unique club was formed primarily to give pilots from the Thud wings a chance to get together and discuss tactics and how to improve them. The idea of the River Rats came from the famed CO of the 8th TFW, Robin Olds. The association took its name from the notorious Red River, which ran from Lao Cai on North Vietnam's border with China, through Yen Bai below Thud Ridge, Phu Tho, and other towns before reaching Hanoi, through which it flowed to the Gulf of Tonkin, effectively cutting the northern part of Vietnam diagonally in half. On and around the Red River were the most dangerous targets, and the name was highly appropriate.

The Rats were actually started by Colonel Howard "Scrappy" Johnson, deputy/388th Wing commander for operations during 1966–67, following Robin Olds's initial fighter-pilot get-together at Ubon early in 1967. Johnson sold the idea to Willy Chairsell, and these two officers planned a dining-in at Korat to launch the Rats. Everyone who had flown a mission into Route Pack Six was invited, but of course the war tended to get in the way of such social events. Many of the guests who qualified had long gone from the theater, and on a grimmer note other would-be members were sitting out the war in North Vietnamese POW compounds.

Nevertheless, the invitations went out. The gathering was open to all who had risked their all in Route Pack VI and took place on 22 May 1967. To make it a lot more than a tactics conference, Korat played host to a bevy of pretty Thai girls and laid on courtesy C-47s to bring the jocks in. As if that were not enough, the home of the Avis Wing held a parade, complete with elephants. Riding atop the beasts were such Red River alumni as Robin Olds and "Blackman," alias Chappie James, fellow F-4 driver and one of the few Negroes to reach command status in the USAF at that time. The 13th Air Force band provided the music, and by midafternoon the conference was in full swing.

By evening, when the serious business of the day was all but complete, the venue changed to the Korat Officers' Club. A bout of alcoholic revelry put the seal on the association, the name was duly toasted to excess, and a good time was had by all present. A firm resolution was made to hold another conference in August, and to continue such meetings at intervals of about three months. It was agreed initially that the River Rats would convene at a different Thai fighter base for the duration of combat

flying over Vietnam, but in fact the association took on
a far greater responsibility, which would lead to annual
gatherings in the US every year following 1969. The
RRVFPA would return to Korat in 1968.

While the Red River was an apt focus for an association
of fighter pilots, the higher route packs held many targets
that had not been intensively attacked by mid-1967. All
too often a first strike had been the only strike, leaving
the enemy to feverishly undertake repairs. It quickly became obvious that the rain of bombs had to be constant,
not sporadic, if the North Vietnamese were to be left
isolated on the battlefields of South Vietnam. Always
there was a requirement for air strikes to place more
bombs more accurately on each target to knock it out.
And always the US fighter pilots faced heavy defenses,
which usually achieved some depletion of forces and
reduced the weight and accuracy of bombs.

F-105 attrition rate, while gradually rising, kept looking statistically reasonable as the sortie rate accumulated.
The problem for the 388th and 355th Wings was that the
supply of low-time F-105D and F models was at best
modest. Despite this, there was no really critical shortage
of aircraft, and by the time both Korat- and Takhli-based
outfits were forced to reduce the number of Thuds that
each squadron maintained, the gap was being closed by
F-4 units. Human stress was eased by squadron rotations,
so that individual pilots could if necessary intersperse
some of the toughest missions with sorties into the lower
route packs to reduce the pressure a little. New pilots
were continually being posted to the combat wings, and
these men needed a short period of "theater indoctri-

nation'' before being sent north, where inexperience could be as great an enemy as the SAMs and AAA.

Even so, the fund of experience was hardly oversubscribed. It seemed to take a particular type of individual application to survive all that the enemy could do and come back for more. Any pilot who completed his statutory hundred missions and volunteered for further tours was therefore very valuable indeed. He could pass on his firsthand experience to the newcomers and explain the rules, few of which could be gleaned from textbooks, for they were continually changing.

But if there was one thing that united the great majority of pilots tasked with taking the war into the North during Rolling Thunder, it was the F-105. Although their mission was primarily what later came to be somewhat derisively labeled ''mud moving,'' they mostly flew alone in an aircraft with a capital F in front of its number designation. For most, that was enough. Weasel drivers, often but not always part of a two-man crew, could be grouped with F-4 crews in the crew numbers game—but it might have been safer not to. Weasel flyers were a breed apart, fighter pilots with a big plus.

To a man, they had the greatest regard for the Thud. ''Lead Sled,'' ''Squash Bomber,'' ''Ultra Hog''—it seemed that the more derogatory the epithet, the more the mighty Republic fighter came through for its crews. The company had built a reputation for big, tough airplanes in World War II, when the P-47 Thunderbolt staggered many with its sheer bulk. The F-105 carried on that tradition, and nobody who had to take it into combat wanted a lighter, flimsier mount. With aerial refueling constantly on hand, the Thailand-based Thud Wings could fly fast all day if necessary.

It was a well-known fact that Thud drivers rated their machine over the newer—and very widely publicized—F-4. On MiGCAPs the Phantoms would maneuver almost "clean," having dropped even their long-range fuel tanks to stay with the nimble NVAF MiGs. But F-105s went into battle loaded down with ECM pods, long-range tanks, and racks full of bombs. Pilots were not encouraged to jettison their fuel tanks or ECM pods, and they could still fight MiGs on equal terms.

Such claims might be disputed by Phantom crews who rightly believed that they had a superlative airplane, and nobody should get the idea that every example of a mass-produced F-105 or F-4 was the same. But the F-105 pilot had two things in his favor and for which F-4 crews had few counters. One was that the F-105D had one seat; two, that it had been designed to carry a gun, so it was a "true" fighter pilot's fighter. During Rolling Thunder, most F-4 kills were with missiles rather than the gun pods with which the aircraft was belatedly fitted in 1966. Not until the advent of the F-4E was there a Phantom with a gun built into the airframe, and many F-105 exponents believed their aircraft was a far superior firing platform than any F-4 with one or more pods. Finally, any such argument could be settled by the Thud pilot simply by noting that when he made a MiG kill, he did it without the help of another man in the back seat. When F-4 back-seaters were credited with air-to-air kills on equal status with the aircraft commander, even the pro-F-4 lobby rebeled. The question remained controversial throughout the SE Asian war and even beyond.

In reality, these topics remained in the realms of healthy rivalry. Both the F-105 and F-4 were among the world's best tactical combat aircraft, and, like any good team, they needed each other. Provided that flights could maintain formation, a force composed of multiple F-4 MiGCAP aircraft, Wild Weasel and/or Iron Hand F-105s and F-105 bombers could inflict heavy damage and reduce the defenses by one or more radar installations and if possible a number of guns and SAMs. By pinpointing known gun and missile sites and allocating a proportion of the strike force bombers as flak suppressors, the USAF was invariably able to hurt the enemy badly by use of deadly CBU bombs. These weapons contained hundreds of tiny ball bearings that spread out from the main streamlined bomb casing on impact and sliced through hard and soft targets with ballistic force.

By June 1967, two of the original 388th TFW squadrons remained at Korat—as they would for the duration of the war—and these had been joined by others on rotation from the 355th Wing at Takhli. This pattern remained pretty much in force throughout the Air Force's tenure in Thailand. It had brought the 44th Tactical Fighter Squadron, the "Vampires," to Korat on 25 April, to replace the 421st, which went back to the States for two years before reassignment to South Vietnam. The Vampires were transferred from the 18th TFW based at Kadena on Okinawa.

Thus in mid-1967, the 388th had the 13th, 34th, 44th, and 469th Squadrons assigned, there being a fifth flight within the jurisdiction of the 13th TFS to handle the Wild Weasel mission with F-105Fs, widely but unofficially designated "EF-105Fs" to distinguish their ECM ca-

pability from standard two-seat F models. All these
squadrons would supply available aircraft for strike missions, and it was not unusual for a unit as small as a
flight to be drawn from different squadrons. At this period, the Air Force Wings in Thailand were still flying
aircraft that had no obvious distinguishing markings apart
from the serial number. Pilots and, where appropriate,
back-seaters personalized individual Thuds and flew them
whenever they were on line for mission availability. The
pace of the war meant that this was not always possible,
and it did happen that a pilot's "regular" aircraft would
be taken on a mission by someone else, only to be posted
as missing in action. Despite this ever-present risk, aircraft became associated with individual pilots, just as
they had been in previous conflicts.

   An observer witnessing a strike sortie getting under
way at Korat in 1967 might therefore have a feeling of
déjà vu if he realized how widely known some of the
names given to warplanes had become in conflicts past.
To some extent, the same thing was happening in this
war.

   If our observer was at Korat on 5 June 1967, he could
well have seen the following typical mix of F-105Ds: 60-
497 "Miss T" of the 44th TFS, an aircraft handed down
by the 421st, a fact indicated by red trim and the shade
of paint used for the name (red was the 421st squadron
color, while the 44th TFS initially used black and, subsequently, blue). Representing the 34th TFS on that date
were six F-105Ds: 60-449, "Bounty Hunter"; 59-1760,
"War Lord II"; 61-0132, "Hanoi Special"; 61-0124,
"Eight Ball"; 61-0205, "Mr. Blackbird"; and 61-0194,
"The Avenger."

Our hypothetical flightline watcher would have had to
have been quite close to each aircraft to read its name,
for each was, as related previously, tucked away under
the wing root. Of all these Thuds, the most famous was
to be "Hanoi Special," which was the regular mount of
1 Lt David B. Waldrop III and in due course became a
double MiG-killer. On a more sobering note, which
serves to illustrate the attrition rate exacted by Vietnam
combat on the Thud wings, had our man checked the F-
105 tail numbers again one year later, he'd have found
that five of the aircraft "logged" in June 1967 had been
written off. Of the seven, only "Bounty Hunter" was to
survive the Air Force's entire period of combat in SE
Asia. The term "written off" could mean that the aircraft
in question was shot down or had been so badly damaged
as to be fit only for the scrap pile; alternatively, it could
have succumbed on a training flight or other operationally
related sortie.

In May 1967, the 388th's rival Wing at Takhli had
been honored with its first Presidential Unit Citation for
its achievements over a ten-month period the previous
year. In June it was announced that the "Hertz" crowd
had also recorded the first 2,000-flying-hours mark by a
single F-105. The Korat-based Wing was suitably un-
impressed until July, when the 469th could announce that
hard flying was far from the sole prerogative of the 355th
by logging no less than 20,000 hours since it had begun
combat in December 1965. Subsequently, both F-105
Wings were to boast similar figures for combat hours—
and official recognition of their efforts. The 388th's first
PUC was followed by a second Air Force Outstanding
Unit Award with Combat "V" Device (AFOUA/V) for

the period 1 July 1966 to 30 June 1967, upon presentation of which that summer, the Wing had flown 56,000 combat hours.

This high number meant that many pilots flying Thuds had completed their primary hundred-missions requirement—for which, incidentally, they were presented with a special certificate by Republic Aircraft—and by mid-1967, this figure had exceeded two hundred. At that time (May 1967) the Air Force announced that it had 406 of the total (all models including those that were not cleared for combat) 833 F-105s built remaining on strength, the great majority then being stationed in Thailand and comprising D and F models.

6

THROUGHOUT the war against North Vietnam, by far the most difficult targets for TAC fighter bombers had been bridges. They had constantly to be hit to undo the repair work the enemy always seemed able to accomplish. Even as the sound of the last attacking F-105 faded away, an army of people descended on the site, picked its way around the still-smoking bomb craters, and set to. Often the job wasn't completed in weeks or even months; it all depended on how much damage the US air strikes had been able to inflict.

The Air Force found that 500- and 750-lb iron bombs could indeed drop supporting spans into the rivers and severely shake the concrete pillars, but it usually took a great many bombs and risked a lot of airplanes to the defenses. One answer was to use bigger bombs and, as Willy Chairsell completed his eleven-month tenure as CO of the 388th on 31 August, plans were being laid to widen

the target list again. This time the Thailand-based Wings
would be able to hit a vital link on the North Vietnamese
rail net and one that hitherto had been frustratingly "off
limits." The target was the Paul Doumer bridge, close
to Hanoi and the longest in North Vietnam.

Chairsell handed over to CO Ed Burdett on 1 August,
and under his leadership the 388th contributed to a new
daily high-sortie rate launched on 3 August. Numerous
targets were attacked, and on the 8th, the new Rolling
Thunder target list was announced. Four days later, the
initial Paul Doumer bridge strike was fragged to the strike
squadrons.

The exacting art of bridge-busting had always called
for the highest degree of skill and courage, as the enemy
always defended these vital road and rail links with tenacity. The mid-1960s Thud drivers, had they been able
to talk to fighter and medium bomber pilots from World
War II and Korea about bridge strikes, would have found
that the problems in achieving permanent closure were
much the same. In Vietnam, though, the concentration
of guns around bridges brought added problems to a job
that was difficult to begin with.

Pilots quickly came to recognize what caliber of guns
formed the defense ring by the color and size of the bursts
streaming up as they screamed down. There was white
for the 37mm, gray for 57s, and big black bursts with
red centers to mark a nest of 85mm to 100mm weapons
that could claw down an F-105 up to an altitude of 40,000
feet. On a strike, few Thuds would be that high. Down
in the weeds was perhaps even more dangerous, but a
low run would probably place the bombs more accurately
and do lasting damage, enough at least for another strike

to be unnecessary tomorrow or the next day, or the day after that. It was reckoned by the best exponents of bridge attack that a release altitude of 3,500 feet would do the trick. From that height, impacts could be observed and any corrections passed to the next flight in.

While the decision to attack the Paul Doumer bridge was long overdue, other bridges had been on the Rolling Thunder target list for over three years. Indeed, it was from Korat in the days before the creation of the 388th that Lieutenant Colonel Robinson Risner's 67th TFS made the first Air Force strike on the notorious Thanh Hoa bridge, on 1 April 1965. The Thanh Hoa, or "Dragon's Jaw," defied all attempts by the USAF and Navy to put it permanently out of commission, but it was badly damaged on the follow-up 2 April raid and others that followed. Other bridges succumbed to the rain of Air Force and Navy bombs, but not the Dragon's Jaw. Its time would come, but it was not to be during Rolling Thunder.

The August 1967 target-list revision, Rolling Thunder 57, contained six located within a ten-mile radius of downtown Hanoi, and the Paul Doumer bridge had high priority. It had originally served as the rail entry point to Hanoi for both the east (Haiphong) and west (Lao Cai) lines, but by mid-1967 had grown in importance to service feeder lines from Kep, Thai Nguyen, and Dong Dang to the north. The bridge was 5,532 feet long and thirty-eight feet wide, with a one-meter railway track in the center flanked by ten-foot-wide highways on each side. The bridge was supported by eighteen massive concrete piers with ten thru-thrust spans, eight of which were 350 feet wide and two 250 feet. Nine cantilever spans were each 246 feet long. Including the 2,935 feet of the approach viaducts, the entire length of the structure was 6,467 feet.

Aware of the fact that even guided ordnance in the form of the Navy's AGM-62 Walleye glide bomb had failed to give the Dragon's Jaw a knockout punch, Air Force mission planners for the Doumer bridge strikes specified much heavier bombs. It was decided to try M-118 3,000-pounders, two of which could be carried by the F-105.

When a strike was scheduled for a given day, headquarters would normally inform the bases the day before so that adequate time was available to fuel and arm the aircraft for early-morning takeoff. This time-consuming job involved loading specific bombs and other munitions, arming the M-61 guns, and fueling and installing electronic equipment. Consequently, when the frag order for the bridge strike was received at Korat and the other Thai bases, the F-105s and F-4s already stood poised to launch, loaded with 750-lb bombs. In order to get the strike airborne in the clear morning conditions before the oppressive midday heat, line crews would normally have their work cut out: it was not standard procedure to load munitions onto fully fueled airplanes. But it became apparent that this was no routine mission when permission was granted to take off the 750-pounders and attach the big bombs. A job that normally took one hour per aircraft was accomplished in eighteen minutes.

As the order for the bridge attack had not been received earlier than 1000 hours, there was little choice but to launch early in the afternoon. Fortunately, the weather forecast en route and over the target promised excellent conditions, and the crews had plenty of time to prepare for takeoff around 1400. Similar ordnance-changing activity took place at Korat.

The strike was to be led by the 355th's Colonel Bob White, who acted as force commander and mission leader, with twenty F-105s. An equal number of Thuds was provided by the 388th, and the Wolfpack fielded four flights of four F-4Cs for MiGCAP and flak suppression. In addition, there was one flight of F-105Fs for Wild Weasel duty.

In the event, the Paul Doumer bridge strike got underway at 1418. Time-on-target had been set for 1558, and the mission worked backward so that engine start took place at precisely 1350. It took less than four minutes to launch the Thud strike force, each aircraft lifting off at eleven-second intervals after a ground roll of just over one mile.

At Korat, the Weasel element of the 388th's force was led by Lieutenant Colonel Jim McInerney, who commanded the 44th TFS at that time. He and his backseater, Captain Fred Shannon, had a spectacular day by destroying six SAM sites and damaging four others. The sortie brought Jim McInerney—whose brother Tom was on the Doumer bridge strike riding a Wolfpack Phantom—an Air Force Cross. Fred Shannon was similarly honored.

With no aborts due to mechanical malfunction, the strike force joined up to head for point Green Anchor, the refueling rendezvous over Laos. In such hot and high conditions (it was approaching 100°C over Thailand on takeoff), the F-105s burned a lot of fuel. It was standard operating procedure to ensure that tankers orbited as close as possible to North Vietnam in order to keep all active strike elements fully topped off. Laden as they were with two 3,000-lb bombs on each inboard wing pylon, the Thuds were heavy; individual aircraft also burn fuel at different consumption rates, and it was necessary for some a little "down on the gauges" to hit the tankers right after forming up.

On crossing into North Vietnam, the Thud flights "greened up," meaning that all switches were set for ordnance release. Out ahead, the Weasels were conducting their electronic search for active radars. The force went from 500 kts to about 600 as it traversed the Red River at 10,000 feet. Some ninety-five miles northwest lay Hanoi.

A turn, and the Thuds and Phantoms were chasing their shadows down Thud Ridge, the distinctive line of low hills that had, due to Air Force insistence that similar ingress routes be repeatedly used, been the graveyard of far too many F-105s. As they came on, the North Vietnamese gunners attempted to lock on their sights. But acquiring such fast-moving targets was one thing; shooting them down was quite another. At Mach 0.9, the US force was visible for mere seconds. On this occasion, as before, rapid altitude changes were made to throw the gunners off their aim. Nevertheless, the flak came up thick and fast. MiGs also scrambled from Phuc Yen airfield, but they were too late. Their hastily executed turns to come in ahead of the US machines achieved nothing, and to reverse and pursue was a waste of time.

At the eastern end of Thud Ridge, the mighty Paul Doumer was clearly visible against a backdrop of Red

River currents. The force made its "pop up" to 13,000 feet both to evade the low-altitude flak and form up separate attack flights. At a point chosen to be the correct one for a 45-degree dive angle, the flights went into echelon. Pilots trimmed their aircraft for the final plunge on those bridge spans. Massive close up, they looked mighty small from 13,000 feet, and the AAA crews were not making the task any simpler.

Rolling in, each F-105 pilot saw, out of the corner of his eye, the flak-suppressor ships going to work. North of the river, an 85mm site simply disappeared in a massive explosion. In each cockpit the stick was pushed forward as the instrument dials whirled and the nose dropped. It took about seven seconds to complete the dive. Seven seconds that seemed like seven days in that welter of exploding steel.

Flight lead released bombs from 8,000 feet, 550 kts IAS. His wingman waited for another thousand to unwind and pickled his load. Speed brakes in. Turn and head downriver, east toward downtown Hanoi. Into burner, each egressing Thud made a morale-boosting sonic boom for the men incarcerated in the Hanoi Hilton.

Looking back, the strike pilots saw one span of the Paul Doumer bridge go down. Immediately the code word "Giraffe" was flashed: the mission had been a success. As the smoke from the initial hits cleared, the 388th went in, as did the few 8th Wing F-4s configured as bombers. More hits. Two highway spans on the northeast side of the bridge were blown away, and the highway portion on the north side was cut at the point where it ran over a small island in the river. In total, thirty-six F-105s had dropped ninety-four tons of bombs in order to stop nearly 6,000 short tons of rail supplies from reaching their destination.

Heading the 388th's strike force that day was Lieutenant Colonel Harry W. Schurr of the 469th. He later described the 3,000-pounders carried by the Thuds as bursting like big orange balls as they struck the bridge. Amazingly, only two F-105s were damaged; both took flak hits but were able to reach Thailand. One aircraft was wrecked on landing, but the pilot walked away from it.

Considering the size of the force, the Paul Doumer strike was one of the most successful to date. That fact was reflected in the message Lieutenant General Momyer flashed to the bases of the Wings involved. In part it read: "[The attack] was a display of the finest bombing and teamwork witnessed to date in the SEA conflict."

Soon after this strike, the weather closed in, greatly assisting the North Vietnamese in their repair work. Unreliable at best, the weather could hamper US air strikes for weeks on end, and it was not until the fall of 1967 that the Paul Doumer figured once more in the target lists. Unfortunately, it was rare that even excellent bombing such as that of 11 August could cause lasting damage. And once a target had been attacked, it was almost inevitable that the enemy would prepare a hot reception for whenever the US airplanes returned. At best, Air Force planners could hope for only a two- to three-month interruption in the flow of North Vietnamese supplies before the same job had to be done all over again. So it was for the Paul Doumer bridge, but considering its location and the sheer weight of firepower expended to protect it, Air Force casualties were remarkably light.

In August 1967, there was another series of intensive air strikes on the North. Missions were planned to take advantage of the prevailing weather, and a week before the Paul Doumer bridge attack the Air Force undertook 197 sorties in a single day (3 August), the highest in a twenty-four-hour period since 4 October 1966. With more targets released under the recently expanded list, both new and old locations were bombed. Sorties during this period took the Thunderchief Wings ever closer to North Vietnam's border with China—a mere ten miles on 14 August, when a railroad bridge at Ki Kung was hit. At that time, the fear was less of direct Chicom intervention in the war than the loss of trained aircrews who might have little choice, either through battle damage or air combat with NVNAF MiGs, but to stray over the border.

The month also brought signs that the widespread damage and interdiction by Air Force and Navy aircraft was causing concern to the enemy. Certain areas of Hanoi began to evacuate nonessential personnel (those who had little or no direct involvement in the war effort) on the 25th. Otherwise, there was no sign that the US and North Vietnam would be able to negotiate a successful cease-fire. On the contrary, as the year progressed, Ho Chi Minh's regime began planning an enormous gamble aimed at reuniting the two Vietnams under communist rule.

As had happened before, MiG activity remained patchy: many US air strikes were left to run the substantial enough gauntlet of AAA and SAMs without aerial opposition. It was widely reckoned that the Operation Bolo success of the previous January had proved so traumatic to the NVNAF that it dared not expose itself to such a relatively high loss risk unless it had absolute local air superiority. Realistically, the Vietnamese squadron commanders knew that they would be very lucky ever to achieve that situation. Technically, the US had always had a big lead on the opposing MiG force, and by 1967 the gap was growing wider.

That was not, of course, to say that the enemy MiG force could be ignored, as the 388th found out on 23 August. Fortunately, the clash of arms resulted in another US victory, but this was offset by the loss of two F-4s to MiG-21s. A wild dogfight ensued, with F-4Cs and Ds, F-105s, MiG-17s, and MiG-21s tussling over Yen Vien, dangerously close to downtown Hanoi's defenses. This action came a week after Lieutenant General Momyer's widely quoted pronouncement that previous air actions had all but cleared MiGs from the skies.

Unknown to the United States, the NVNAF had been planning new tactics while bringing fresh pilots up to combat status and continuing their ongoing training program. Hit-and-run attacks had always been favored by the enemy simply because the lack of a high number of aircraft and well-trained pilots made such interceptions more economical. With low risk to men and machines, the NVNAF would send up a small number of MiG-17s or -21s, which would charge in on American strike flights and, it was hoped, force one or more F-105s to jettison their ordnance. Similar tactics were employed on 23 August.

Barely had anyone had time to call a warning before two Atoll AAMs took out two Phantoms. MiG-21s had shadowed the force from high cloud cover and made their attack from 25,000 feet. It was doubly unfortunate that the lack of recent MiG interceptions had led to an increase in F-4s configured as strike bombers rather than MiGCAP fighters. That day only one flight of F-4s from the 8th TFW flew in the MiGCAP role, and it was two Wolfpack aircraft that were downed. Three good 'chutes were observed, however, as the Russian missiles found their mark.

The balance of the strike force for Yen Vien was made up of five flights of Korat's F-105s: three on strike, one of flak suppression/strike, and one Iron Hand flight. The intercept took place after the target had been bombed and was a variation on an established pattern employed by the MiG pilots. Now it appeared that they would approach the US aircraft at low level, go into a maximum power climb, and make a single firing pass, using available cloud cover. Not seeking to tangle with the American escort, the MiGs then made an equally fast exit and hightailed it for their home bases or one of a number of alternate fields over the border in China.

Up that day was "Hanoi Special," the F-105D in the capable hands of First Lieutenant David Waldrop, III, who was on his fifty-third mission. Using the call sign Crossbow 3, Waldrop had a successful day. He was convinced that by the time the combat was over, he had destroyed two enemy fighters.

Waldrop's initial engagement was with a MiG-17 soon after he had bombed the designated target. He saw a pair of them below his aircraft as he executed a roll to the right. One of the MiGs was intent on a Thud and apparently failed to see his pursuer. Waldrop broke in on this MiG, went into burner, and closed in. He fired his cannon, and the MiG seemed to have been hit in the wing. Fire was observed at the tips and at midpoint before the enemy fighter slow-rolled to the right. Waldrop dropped back and fired again. The MiG continued to roll right into the ground and blew up.

This action was observed from above by Colonel Robin Olds in a Wolfpack Phantom. Olds was moved to comment that the MiG–F-105 duel looked to him like a "shark chasing a minnow." Olds even saw the MiG fall; but despite this supporting evidence of Waldrop's prowess, the claim was denied.

Also disappointed was Major Billy Givens, flying as Crossbow lead. He engaged a MiG after leaving the target, letting it have more than nine hundred rounds of 20mm to at least make the pilot lose interest in the Thud he was chasing. Givens was certain that the MiG had been damaged, and initially he was credited with a probable. This, too, was later denied by the Seventh Air Force Claims Evaluation Board, which did not list anything but definite kills.

Givens and Waldrop then picked up two more MiG-17s, the latter pilot firing at a range of 3,000 feet with 85-degree angle-off. The fighters were then at 7,500 feet. With three hundred rounds gone, Waldrop stopped firing at 2,500 feet separation, having observed hits. He rolled out and headed west with his Thud inverted, his intention being to see clearly what happened to this MiG after it dived into cloud. Reemerging from cloud, the MiG immediately had the F-105 on his tail again, and this time, despite a gunsight malfunction, Waldrop made sure. Down to 6,500 feet altitude, the American closed to 2,000 feet and pumped 250 20mm rounds into the MiG's fuselage, working the stick so that his shells impacted the canopy area and traveled back toward the tail. The MiG promptly exploded, rolled inverted, and hit the ground. Waldrop recovered at 3,500 feet and egressed the combat area.

Back at Korat, Waldrop was understandably convinced that he had scored two victories and was initially credited with them officially. Subsequently, the review board validated only the second claim.

Overall, 23 August was not a good day for the Air Force. Although the enemy had lost at least one aircraft and a pilot, the consensus was that the strike force should never have been jumped. The intelligence system as worked by headquarters creaked more than usual, and Olds's Wolfpack was not told that new MiG interception tactics were strongly suspected. The day's final result was a badly damaged F-105 and the loss of no fewer than four Phantoms.

David Waldrop's confirmed F-105D MiG kill was the last for the 388th of that type of aircraft, and only three more Thud kills were made throughout the remainder of the US involvement in SE Asia. The Korat Wrecking Crew would get back among the air victories, but in Phantoms—in more ways than one, the end of an era was approaching.

7

THE fall of 1967 saw Rolling Thunder air strikes rise to a Vietnam war peak; the F-105 Wings in Thailand attacked a wide range of targets, the majority of them aimed at cutting rail and road links and destroying trains and rolling stock in yards. Interspersed with 7th Fleet Navy attacks, the 388th and 355th Wings went all out to convince North Vietnam, not to mention its Chinese and Russian allies, that continuation of the war was futile.

With a total land area exceeding 40,000 square miles, North Vietnam's primary industries consisted of coal mining, zinc phosphates, tin and graphite, and cement. Relatively little of this production was exported to countries other than those of a communist persuasion, and the country's rice crop was, particularly after the start of the war, used almost exclusively to feed the population, rather than to supply other nations. The North was there-

fore a country that, on the face of it, was susceptible to
economic isolation if her indigenous industries were
badly disrupted and her sources of outside help block-
aded. But just as South Vietnam had drawn on the vast
resources of the US, so Ho Chi Minh was unlikely to
bleed white those of China and Russia. The slim chance
of widening the rift between the two Asiatic superpowers
and persuading either of them that North Vietnam was a
lost cause as long as she continued to seek unification
under communist rule was explored diplomatically by the
US. It took time to woo China, and it was not until
Richard Nixon moved into the White House in November
1968 that progress began to be made.

In the meantime, the thunder rolled on. A groundswell
of antiwar protest was rising in the US, and for their
part, many American airmen, who were the military
spearhead of political failure to agree to peace terms, or
indeed to win the war, wondered just how many more
lives it was going to take. With the number of sorties
already flown and the weight of bombs dropped on North
Vietnam, the war had already exceeded the Korean War
on both counts. Men wondered if it was going to drag
on longer than World War II and questioned just what
they were supposed to be trying to achieve in fighting a
war with one hand tied behind their backs.

But in late 1967, nobody could answer such questions.
Reason seemed hardly to have a say. Pilots who on almost
a daily basis saw better than any office-bound planner
thousands of miles from the action what targets to hit
and how hard to hit them, found their suggestions ignored. At worst, these intelligent, up-to-the-minute sum-
maries of the tactical situation were treated almost as

treasonable offenses by certain high-ranking officers who should have known better. Pilots found it better to shut up and just keep trying to do what amounted to the near-impossible.

While most Rolling Thunder strikes—those that involved multiple flights of F-105s and F-4s—were carried out in daylight, it did not pass unnoticed in USAF planning circles that the enemy could accomplish much during the hours of darkness. Much effort was therefore expended by all branches of the US services to "deny the enemy the night." A substantial number of systems and techniques were combat-tested in Vietnam, ranging from highly demanding blacked-out helicopter attacks to sophisticated night-vision equipment that could "see" personnel, vehicles, and installations even in the inky blackness that descended over jungle terrain as soon as the sun went down.

Traditionally, the USAF and its forebears had been largely a daylight combat force, although previous conflicts had by necessity spawned an efficient night-fighter element to deal with enemy aircraft. Attacking ground targets at night, particularly with modern high-performance jets, was something else. But again the Vietnam War saw the successful development of such operations. They were among the most demanding and specialized missions flown, requiring a high degree of pilot skill coupled with a razor-sharp human brain in the back seat of the F-105F or F-4 to interpret, with lightning speed, the degree of threat from NVA ground defenses. Thus were born "Ryan's Raiders."

Grouped under the generic code name "Commando Nail," nocturnal strike missions were rarely called that.

Instead, the nickname picked up following instigation of such missions by PACAF chief John D. Ryan proved far more popular. Apart from the cloak of darkness, North Vietnam, in common with other areas of SE Asia, was subject to what amounted to two seasons rather than four. These were the northeast and southwest monsoons. The former brings the November-to-March "dry" season, and the latter the April-to-October "rainy" period. And anyone familiar with that part of the world knows that "rainy" means just that—the stuff falls in torrents for hours on end, leaving a sticky, humid atmosphere at ground level and dense mist in the sky. The latter also provided ideal cover for enemy activity and often prevented visual identification of targets for daylight strikes. Ryan's Raiders therefore had a dual night/bad weather mission, and the job was handed to the 44th TFS at Korat in the spring of 1967.

The Raider mission had its roots in tests with the B-58, which aimed to give SAC's supersonic long-range bomber the capability to deliver iron bombs as well as nuclear weapons. But by 1967 the Hustler's days in service were numbered, and added to the risk of exposing such a costly airplane to North Vietnam's defenses, the idea was not feasible. The pinpoint inclement weather/night attack mission would not be fully explored under combat conditions until the F-111's second SE Asian combat debut in 1972. Meanwhile, the "tried and tested" F-105 partially filled the gap.

Ryan's Raider F-105Fs did not fly the Wild Weasel mission but had their R-14A radar tuned to expand 'scope presentation and give a sharper target definition. Some modification was made to the pilot's weapon-release switch to enable the rear-seat electronics warfare officer, universally dubbed "the Bear," to control bomb release. Such missions were extremely hazardous radar-controlled bombing sorties in pairs or full Flight strength, usually with a couple of Weasels along to deal with any Fire Can or Fan Song radars that might pick up the prowling Thuds.

Many pilots got hooked on the night mission, despite the hazards. They were often the only aircraft flying, and any light source would invariably be the work of the bad guys. Not all guns needed radar prediction, and if they had the range, the NVA gunners could catch a Raider unawares with a sudden burst of barrage fire. But if they missed, the gunflashes would draw the F-105s like moths to a candle flame; unless they stayed quiet and left the potential targets naked, the enemy had to give away his position. A night SAM shot could also be seen for miles.

Another addition to the F-105's night repertoire was the Combat Martin F model. Fitted with QRC-128 VHF jammers, these aircraft were able to blot out communications between airborne MiGs and their ground controllers. The enemy invariably flew short-range missions under ground control interception (GCI) direction, which helped to overcome a general level of pilot inexperience. Other aircraft, particularly EB-66s and EC-121s, supported Rolling Thunder air strikes throughout the campaign, although radio- and radar-jamming missions had to be carefully coordinated once the F-105s began using ECM equipment as a routine aid to survival. The powerful transmitters aboard the Destroyers and Constellations were quite capable of blotting out all communications, friendly or enemy, if their respective orbits overlapped the electronic screen of a strike force.

Although the available inventory of F-105s distributed between the Korat and Takhli Wings steadily declined throughout Rolling Thunder, there had been some remarkable "saves" of battle-damaged aircraft, and both the Air Force and Republic wanted detailed data on resultant airframe stress that might prove useful, both for the immediate prosecution of the war and to assist in the design of future combat aircraft. Thought was given to reopening the Thunderchief production line, as there was still little to match its performance even as Rolling Thunder reached its 1967 climax. This decision was not taken, and instead, a technical evaluation team set out to determine just how rugged the F-105 was.

They started this process by instrumenting six Korat aircraft and six from Takhli early in 1966. What Air Force Logistics Command engineers wanted to know was how often, and by how much, airframe load limitations were approached—or exceeded—during the rigors of "average" combat missions. It could be said that flying over North Vietnam was never average, but the data the aircraft produced made interesting reading, compressing as it did a mass of information that would only accrue from normal Stateside flying over a long period, into a few months.

Understandably, there was no method of ensuring that the instrumented Thuds survived, and it was not long before ten out of twelve were out of commission or lost. Another attempt was made in mid-1966. Seven aircraft were instrumented this time, and between 14 August 1966 and 29 April 1967, 3,055 hours of combat time were logged. Primarily the instruments recorded imposed G loads and the degree of air pressure on the airframe throughout each flight.

It was found that while each F-105 was taking off at a loaded weight below that of the design maximum (between 49,500 and 50,900 lb), the loads imposed during combat maneuvering were regularly being exceeded. The F-105D was stressed to withstand 8.67 G when maneuvering subsonically and 7.33 G supersonically. North Vietnam's defenses obliged flight profiles up to 10.3 G, the maximum recorded during this combat trial.

It was also revealed that the 388th Wing flew its Thuds harder than the 355th in that Korat F-105s seemed to produce higher G loadings. The 388th supplied eight of the eleven aircraft instrumented for the tests, and one example, 62-4357, drawn from the 34th TFS and named, appropriately, "Thunderchief" by its pilot/crew chief, logged combat loads in excess of 7.5 G no fewer than eighty-nine times during one 1,000-hour period. Shortly after the end of the test phase, on 5 May 1967, this aircraft was written off; but it had, as had so many other F-105s, proven its extreme ruggedness. The next-nearest load-exceeding aircraft had done so thirty-one times during 1,000 flight hours.

The evaluators also found that the 388th tended to land its F-105s at heavier weights—as high as 6.5 G during let-down, and that during the summer of 1967, the Wing achieved a remarkable 99.77 takeoff rate during one month's operation. Across the board, the F-105D's operational availability record was always high, the two Wings based in Thailand achieving an average of seven to eight percent on any given day when the USAF goal for its entire force was set at five percent.

This superb maintenance record under the strain of combat was achieved by round-the-clock, three-shift toil by the able ground crews assigned to the Thud Wings. With their ground-crew complement well above the normal for a TAC Wing, the Korat and Takhli squadrons were assured of adequate aircraft to fulfill every mission, as long as there were aircraft left to maintain. The record was undoubtedly helped by the longevity of the Thud line, many of which were to exceed the average airframe fatigue life of 4,000 hours. Some of the aircraft that reached multiple thousands of hours have been mentioned, and more were to show their durability before the American involvement in Vietnam ended.

Spares availability was not a minus factor during Rolling Thunder; the main F-105 spares center was the Air Materiel Area located at McClellan AFB, in Sacramento, California, and this facility managed a steady flow of parts to the war zone. Pratt and Whitney also met the challenge admirably. To ensure that each F-105 wing had enough J75s on hand and that engines pulled from operational airplanes maintained power, the Thailand Wings changed F-105 power plants at 125-hour intervals instead of the Air Force norm of 200 hours. People began to believe that you actually could throw a rock into one of the Thud's intakes while the engine was running and watch sand trickle out the other end!

Apart from leave and short-duration R & R, the F-105 ground crews had little direct cause to celebrate a job well done, but they were pleased to participate in the party when a pilot completed his one hundred missions.

These men, like countless thousands before them in other wars, sweated out the return of their charges on every sortie. When the aircraft flown by the pilot who had made the coveted century mark touched down, there would invariably be a parade of vehicles to lead it into the hardstanding. When the pilot, alone or accompanied by his rear-seat Bear if it was an F model, stepped onto the ladder to climb down, he was hosed down. It was hot and sweaty in an F-105 cockpit even without the adrenaline of combat, and the soaking was welcome. It mattered not whether the venue was Korat, Takhli, or any other base; the ceremony was much the same. Some pilots were really cooled off by being dumped in the base swimming pool, before or after slaking their thirst with champagne, beer, or whatever was available. It was a surefire method of reminding the man that he had completed his tour. It did not always mean that he'd flown only a hundred missions, for such was the nature of the Vietnam War that sorties into Laos didn't count, even if these amounted to another ten, twenty, or more. And the hosedown didn't necessarily mean that our man would catch the next transport flight out. For some, the lure of combat proved too great, and there were those who qualified for a second soaking. Some titans went on for even more. It all said one hell of a lot for the aircraft they were flying and the kind of men they were.

The gradual improvement in the weather over North Vietnam saw a concurrent increase in air strikes through October. On the 3rd, the F-105s went out after key bridges and those at Loc Binh and Cao Bang were attacked. The following day, it was the turn of the combined highway and railroad crossing at Lang Son and

Chien Chang. On 5 October, the fragged targets included
Kep airfield, Khe Nan and Hoa Lac, plus gasoline-storage
facilities two miles northeast of Haiphong, hit by the
Navy. Among these targets, airfields were perhaps of
greater concern to the pilots, as any MiGs destroyed or
disabled meant that future air strikes could expect slightly
less of a challenge. The enemy air force's relatively small
number of personnel eligible for jet pilot training and the
modest number of aircraft available meant that any disruption to the training program through air attack slowed
the process more in the North Vietnamese Air Force than
many other air arms.

As before, the US target list was wide-ranging and
diversified—too diversified in the opinion of many. But
the required repeat strike on heavily defended factories,
bridges, radar sites, and so forth would undoubtedly have
led to disproportionately higher casualties, or so it was
believed. By again spreading the effort, the resultant
destruction was often only temporary.

Increased capability was continually added to the Korat
and Takhli F-105 force throughout Rolling Thunder. This
behind-the-scenes technical effort was largely aimed at
reducing the effectiveness of North Vietnamese defenses
and included the modification of a small number of F-
105Ds to use the Shrike ARM. These machines operated
with EF-105s and acted as a backup to Weasel flights,
adding their ordnance to antiradar attacks once the two-
seat Thuds had found them. Work to adapt the Navy
Standard ARM to Air Force F-105s did not reach fruition
in 1967, and in fact the Navy itself was not in a position
to deploy the big and highly effective missile to the war
zone before 1968.

In the fall of 1967, further moves were made to give USAF aircraft a better form of air-to-air identification apart from tail numbers. Having introduced camouflage for tactical and other aircraft in 1966, the Air Force gave its aircraft a cloak of anonymity that at times was too effective. Tail codes originated with PACAF, which noted the unit-level measures taken to enhance identification through the use of color trim and more prominent serial numbering. But generally, tactical aircraft remained hard to identify as to parent squadron, Wing or Flight. In the melee of air combat, visual identification was all but impossible.

Thus, the Thailand-based F-105 Wings were issued with a system of two-letter tail codes, which were to be painted above the serial number in light gray. It took time to spray the letters on all aircraft in a Wing, and many Thuds were still flying missions without them well into 1968. The 388th, in common with other combat Wings, had the same letter base code—in this case J— assigned to all squadrons, which were in turn identified by a second letter: JJ for the 34th TFS, JE for the 44th, and JV for the 469th.

At this time some further changes took place at Korat. On 20 October, the 44th TFS absorbed the old 13th TFS to concentrate the Wild Weasel force under one squadron organization. A similar unit at Takhli provided the 355th Wing's Weasel element, this being the detachment that came under the jurisdiction of the 354th TFS.

The last week of October 1967 saw the strike wings hitting another set of targets as the JCS modified the Rolling Thunder list yet again. The period also saw a renewed bout of MiG activity, which prompted a first-time strike on Phuc Yen, the largest jet-capable base in North Vietnam. A large-scale strike was laid on for the 24th, the Air Force element including Thuds from the 388th and 355th Wings, and F-4s from the 8th TFW. Navy aircraft also participated, and the base was duly plastered.

When the results were analyzed it appeared that four MiG-21s, four MiG-17s, and one MiG-15 had been destroyed or badly damaged, and the runways and parking areas had been heavily cratered. A MiG-21 was shot down by the Phantom MiGCAP, and this victory, added to the fact that the anticipated loss rate of three percent of the strike force did not occur, made it a day to remember. No US aircraft were lost.

On the 25th, the F-105s made another attempt to restrict traffic across the Red River by bombing the Paul Doumer and Long Bien bridges. By 30 August, aerial reconnaissance showed that in about three more weeks the damage inflicted on the Paul Doumer bridge on 11 August would have been all but repaired if the work was allowed to continue. The enemy had initiated a rail ferry service to carry some of the materiel previously moved over the bridge, this being located about three and a half miles southeast of the main spans. Sure enough, by 3 October there was evidence that both rail and vehicular traffic was rolling across the Paul Doumer. Bad weather prevented another air strike until the 25th.

This time a smaller force of Thuds, numbering just twenty-one aircraft, succeeded in knocking out two cantilever spans just east of the island, the eastern pier and the highway deck traversing one span. Again the bridge was down but not out.

Between 26 and 30 October, the pressure was maintained. The MiGs appeared, and four more were shot down. But unlike previous occasions when they had come off the worse for wear against US fighters, the NVNAF did not simply fade away. Accordingly, attacks were ordered against all jet-capable airfields north of the 20th parallel. Only Gia Lam, Hanoi's international airport, was left off the target list.

As these missions continued into November, the enemy dispersed aircraft into bases in China, initiated repairs, and took delivery of replacements. Thus, by year's end, the NVNAF inventory had not been numerically reduced by very much. On 6 November, the Avis Wing sent its aircraft against a storage complex located three miles from Hanoi, while a second strike went to the Kep airfield. The MiGs attacked the latter force.

The 388th had more command changes in November. Ed Burdett relinquished command of the Wing on the 17th, and Colonel Jack C. Berger was in charge for four days. Colonel Neil C. Graham then took over, and he was to lead the Wing through early 1968. Along with other TAC commanders, Graham did his job in a period of uncertainty: Would the current series of air strikes be enough to bring progress on the diplomatic front? Was any "battlefield victory" possible in South Vietnam? How much longer would the war last? These and other questions concentrated the collective minds at every level, from Lyndon Johnson down.

The Thais had long been under pressure from the North Vietnamese to deny the US the use of its bases and stop sending troops to fight against their forces in South Vietnam. Thailand resisted such pressure, but could not be

sure that Ho Chi Minh would not launch some kind of
guerrilla assault against the bases being used by the
USAF, or indeed that the North might attempt air attacks.
Accordingly, base defense was stepped up, and on 2
December it was officially announced that US surface-
to-air missiles had been installed.

Throughout the Vietnam air war, MiG tactics were
observed and analyzed to see how the US could circumvent them and better protect its strike forces. By mid-
December it became obvious that the NVNAF was mar-
shaling its MiG-21s and MiG-17s to use their respective
capabilities to the full. With more pilots converting to
the potent MiG-21, it became possible to deploy these
in high-altitude, high-speed passes while the lower-
performance MiG-17s attacked at lower altitudes. The
MiG-21 was also AAM capable, although the numbers
of this type encountered did not amount to a significant
threat. The MiG-21 did, however, have some effect on
US morale, as its appearance often prompted pilots of
strike bombers to jettison their loads, thus achieving the
enemy's main intercept goal.

A series of railroad interdiction strikes was mounted
in mid-December, the Doumer bridge being among the
targets. The year's final Rolling Thunder strikes were
made on 14 and 18 December, both of which succeeded
in reducing the flow of supplies. When the F-105s turned
for home after the last attack, USAF planners estimated
that it would take the enemy about three months to repair
the damage. In fact, the 3,000-lb bombs aimed by the
Thud Wings had been far more effective than the photo
interpreters judged: it was to be the spring of 1968 before
the North Vietnamese were again able to move supplies

across the Red River, and then only by utilizing a pontoon rail bridge more than four miles away from the Paul Doumer. In total, it had taken 177 sorties to close the longest bridge in North Vietnam; 113 of these were by 388th and 355th Wing F-105s, the balance by F-4s and Weasel F-105 sorties. Two US aircraft had been lost to the defenses and sixteen had been damaged.

For the 388th, 1967 rounded out with a visit to Korat of none other than Lyndon Johnson. Confident that the war was moving toward a climax, Johnson spoke to airmen and enlisted men, praising their efforts in the grueling campaign and perhaps implying that Rolling Thunder was putting more pressure on the North than was actually the case. The 1965–68 air strikes against the North will always be linked with the decisions Johnson took over what and what not to bomb. More than a few of those assembled in one of Korat's hangars on that December morning would have been more than pleased to discuss the air war in much more detail. As it was, the men were unanimous in one thing: when Johnson asked about their airplane requirements, they said simply that more F-105s would do nicely.

When Johnson left Korat, it was business as usual for the 388th. Nobody had an inkling of what was about to happen in South Vietnam. The events there would quickly have wide implications for all aspects of the war and the US involvement. As Christmas 1967 approached, the men of the strike squadrons anticipated a short break from combat operations.

8

FOR the squadrons tasked with taking the war to the enemy homeland, January 1968 opened with little outward sign of any changes in tactics. But during the month, there might have been some indication that the enemy was flexing its muscles. Pilots noted that instead of running for the Chinese border, MiGs attacking US strike forces became more aggressive and often made repeat passes on laden fighter bombers. The USAF responded by increasing the number of F-4s configured for MiGCAP duty rather than bombing, and in general more compact, better-protected strike Flights were sent off from the Thai bases. The Weasel crews did their best to even up the odds against the guns and SAMs, but even their specialized, vital role was meddled with by higher authority. Not content with throwing what might have been a quick, almost surgical series of precision air raids into disarray by delaying decisions as to what was required of its pilots, the US high command issued arbitrary orders with seemingly little thought to the consequences. An example came in late 1967.

When they heard about it, the Weasel pilots were horrified. It concerned an effort by 7th Air Force officers to reduce the attrition rate among the F-105 squadrons by ordering that all aircraft, including EF-105s, carry an AIM-9 Sidewinder on the outboard wing pylon. On the face of it, this move looked sound, and a number of F-105Ds did indeed carry and use their AAMs to good effect. Trouble came when the Weasel crews had to compromise their Shrike missile load. All Thuds had only four wing pylons—which was necessitated by the length of its landing gear legs—and only the outboard pylons were wired to take the antiradiation missile, or an AIM-9. Carrying a missile more as an insurance than as a weapon that would invariably be expended in the specialized Weasel role cut effectiveness of the two-seat Thuds by fifty percent. Arguing loud and long, the Weasel units finally persuaded the powers that be that they needed all the Shrikes they could carry in order to do the job of protecting the strike bombers. Unfortunately, something equally frustrating was to follow.

In its infinite wisdom, 7th AF decided that all tactical aircraft flying sorties against North Vietnam would carry ECM pods—including the Wild Weasel birds! Apparently, nobody was capable of understanding that a Weasel F-105 did not need the pods and that even if the crews never activated the pods, they would still lose a stores station under their airplane's short wing.

Despite such absurdities, the Weasels achieved much.

By January 1968, the 13th/44th TFS at Korat and the 354th at Takhli had accounted for eighty-nine SAM sites destroyed and hundreds forced off the air long enough for the strike force to pass that particular nest of vipers unharmed and unharassed. By late 1967, work was well advanced on giving the Weasel crews the ultimate F-105 adaptation to the antiradar role and one that would finally convince decision-makers with little or no grasp of how it worked. This was the F-105G, the "fully dedicated" Wild Weasel Thud model. When mated with the big and brutal Standard ARM, the Thunderchief truly became the scourge of North Vietnam's radar operators.

Before the end of January 1968, the 388th Wing had had two new commanders. Neil Graham was replaced by Colonel Norman P. Phillips on the 19th, and he in turn gave way to Paul P. Douglas, also a colonel, on the 24th.

Douglas brought with him a good deal of time in the fighter business, and his appointment was therefore welcomed by the men of the 388th. The new CO had been a P-47 jock back in World War II, and he delighted the troops by using on his F-105D the name his Thunderbolt had carried in that conflict: the "Arkansas Traveler" rode again on 59-1743, attached to the 34th TFS.

Shortly before the month ended, the Tet Offensive erupted throughout South Vietnam. It represented something of a last-ditch effort by the Vietcong to "reunite" the entire country against the government of General Nguyen Van Thieu. The series of operations that lasted for some three months all but destroyed the Vietcong as an effective guerrilla force. It was widely believed that had the US and South Vietnam followed the Tet Offensive with one of their own, the war would have all but been won. It was not to be.

Television coverage of a small-scale suicide raid on the US embassy in Saigon achieved far more diplomatically for the North Vietnamese than the entire Tet Offensive ever did militarily. The TV pictures convinced many Americans that the war everyone thought was on the verge of a successful conclusion was lost. Instead of an increase in US military action, Tet was the catalyst for a slowdown, withdrawal, and handover of control to the South Vietnamese.

In Thailand, news of the offensive in the South was equally shocking although there was no immediate letup in the bombing. No enemy air offensive materialized, as might have been expected given the avowed aim of the North to win the war by "popular" uprising.

But in January and February, the NVNAF challenged US air strikes on frequent occasions and again took heavy losses: eight MiGs were downed. Sorties from Thailand continued to be the subject of news reports, although the siege of Khe Sanh began to grab the headlines. It would do so until the firebase was finally secured after seventy-one days of the heaviest fighting of the war.

Early 1968 was marked by some of the worst flying weather of Rolling Thunder. Air strikes were flown at a very decreased level, but by March the 388th was able to announce another record when the 469th Squadron became the first unit in Thailand to complete 30,000 combat hours. In that time, the unit had dropped 135,000 tons of bombs on enemy targets.

The same month Colonel Ivan Dethman, who would

subsequently command the Korat strike Wing, brought the first General Dynamics F-111s to Takhli as part of the Combat Lancer operational evaluation. Then in command of the 428th TFS, Colonel Dethman subsequently had the unenviable task of weathering the bad publicity surrounding the disastrous combat debut of the F-111. The small detachment suffered heavy losses as a result of technical failure, a fact blown out of all proportion by the US media. Later, the F-111 returned for a very successful "second debut."

By April the 388th and 355th had passed the 100,000-combat-hours mark during Rolling Thunder, a remarkable achievement. On the 8th, the Korat Wing celebrated its second anniversary in SE Asian operations. In that period it had flown 38,500 sorties and dropped 86,625 tons of munitions on the enemy. The Wing also received a Presidential Unit Citation for missions flown between 10 March and 1 May 1967.

By then, the nature of the air war against North Vietnam had changed radically. On 31 March, the US president had announced the first of a series of bombing restrictions that would see the end of the Rolling Thunder campaign. Effective 1 April, all bombing north of the 20th parallel was stopped. Two days later, the line was moved south to the 19th parallel. This meant that air strikes could take place only in Route Packs I, II, and the southern third of III, effectively sealing off all the worthwhile targets in the North.

Commanders, pilots, and ground crews showed collective amazement at the decision. Anyone who had been at Korat or Takhli for any length of time knew what the stand-down meant: if the war ever got going again in the areas where it might have hurt the enemy most, the defenses would be even worse. This was common enough knowledge. All previous bombing pauses instigated by the US had given the enemy a respite to make good repairs and provide the hottest possible reception to air attack.

But there were indications that if the US ever did have to send its flyers north again, they would be more than able to look after themselves. The first manifestation of a new range of weaponry tailored directly to SE Asian combat was the operational debut of the Standard ARM, on 6 March. But it was the Navy rather than the Air Force that enjoyed this distinction. Dictates from 7th Air Force prevented the 355th's Weasel element from using the new weapon on 8 March, but the first USAF firing in combat was made three days later.

Before the 44th's Korat Weasels could find a worthwhile target for their Standard missiles, the April bombing restriction was in force. While this edict did not stop air strikes across the DMZ, it did carry the rider that none of the new missiles should be fired at targets in the southern areas of the North. The 388th would have to wait.

Restrictions on bombing North Vietnam did not mean that the strike units based in Thailand stood down. There was certainly a slowdown in the pace of operations, and the urgency that had previously pervaded the bases to confirm the maximum number of F-105s and F-4s for a strike north evaporated (to the relief of the hard-pressed air and ground crews). Now and for some time to come, the fighter bombers would answer calls for air support in South Vietnam. And operations designed to dam the flow of men and material into the battle zones down the notorious Ho Chi Minh Trail continued to be flown over those areas of Laos that fed the tributaries of the Trail. A vast amount of firepower was expended on that network of roads, but the US never did succeed in closing it.

Following President Johnson's announcement that he would not seek renomination in the 1968 election campaign, a number of high-level changes were initiated. Secretary McNamara, a prime architect of Rolling Thunder under Johnson's direction, would remain in office for only a few more months, and while some of the old guard would remain, the US voter was clearly going to enforce a change of government. In May, the first signs that Johnson's bombing halt on the North appeared to have made an impression on Vietnamese officials materialized with a meeting in Paris. It quickly became apparent that the negotiators there had a hard task ahead of them, and one that would not be done quickly.

Meanwhile, flying operations from Korat and Takhli continued, the Wings interspersing combat missions with training. New crews needed schooling in the slightly less risky areas of North Vietnam's lower route packs, but in mid-1968 there would not be the ultimate test of "going downtown" into the teeth of the enemy defenses. Aerial surveillance flights were maintained over the hottest target zones, and soon enough there was ample evidence that the North Vietnamese were making the most of the American peace overtures. As predicted, support for hostile action in South Vietnam hardly waned as cargo ships under Russian and Chinese flags, plus those of nonaligned nations and neutral countries, unloaded at ports no longer endangered by US air strikes.

Also on the agenda for 1968 was the issue of American

prisoners of war; appeals to the North Vietnamese for news of the men (mostly pilots) that they had held in captivity since before the start of the US involvement became increasingly urgent as evidence of widespread ill treatment began to emerge. Along with other services and combat units, the 388th had its contingent of POWs in the various prisons located in the North, including notorious Ha Lo, the "Hanoi Hilton."

Always unpredictable, the North Vietnamese began the surprise release of US POWs in 1968, the first group of three arriving in February. Others were to follow, but the majority were destined to sit it out until the cease-fire in 1973. Only then were the full facts behind treatment of prisoners revealed—the beatings, the confessions of guilt extracted under torture, and the general deprivation of almost all men who fell into enemy hands. On the positive side, the good physical shape of most of the men captured stood them in good stead and enabled almost all of the returnees to make a full recovery. By far the worst aspect of a shoot-down out of reach of the efficient US rescue services was injury sustained either by aircraft taking hits in the target area, or by malfunction of ejector seats or other escape methods: overcoming deficiencies in ejector-seat design was one of the most urgent goals the USAF sought.

With the weather over the lower route-pack areas of North Vietnam restricting combat flying for days on end, the F-105 Wings enjoyed some respite from the most dangerous targets. There was, however, plenty of action when the weather did clear, as the enemy sought to extend the defense net of guns and SAMs into the area immediately above the DMZ. Such sites continued to be attacked.

There was also a full-scale, "secondary" war in neighboring Laos, which had in the early days required that USAF fast jets undertake air strikes against enemy supply movement down the Ho Chi Minh Trail. While there were usually ample numbers of jet- and piston-engined attack planes available in South Vietnam, the Thailand-based Wings were frequently called upon to help, particularly since their bases were usually nearer the fighting. Korat and Takhli, therefore, supported small numbers of "Whiplash" missions, which required a Flight of F-105s to be ready on strip alert to fly at short notice on what were called Steel Tiger sorties and, after December 1965, Tiger Hound. Of course, missions into Laos were not without risk, and gradually the planners placed the responsibility for attacks on the small, hard-to-see argets moving down the Trail in the hands of aircraft other than the Thud. For example, truck destruction was more easily accomplished by aircraft with a better loiter time than jets, and apart from the greater risk that slower aircraft faced from the defenses, they were generally more accurate. It was also realized that any F-105s lost or damaged over Laos would erode the strength available for the main task of bombing North Vietnam, a task for which every available D and F model might still be needed.

The weather restrictions on interdiction of the Trail had been overcome to some degree by the introduction of MSQ-77 Skyspot radar in June 1966. Bombing by radar coordinates became a regular feature of Laotian air operations from then on. Much faith was also placed in the Igloo White program, which involved "seeding" areas of known or suspected enemy activity with thousands of sensors able to detect heat sources from vehicles and human beings and transmit information to high-flying EC-121 Constellations, which would alert fighter bombers.

The EC-121 had been an integral part of USAF/Navy operations over North Vietnam and Laos from the earliest days of the war. Known by their code name Rivet Top and, later, Disco, the electronics-crammed derivatives of the old Lockheed airliner gave a sterling airborne early-warning capability. Among the units that carried out these vital tasks was the 553rd Reconnaissance Wing, colocated with the 388th Wing at Korat from 31 October 1967.

For the 388th Wing, as for others, the changed emphasis of combat operations during 1968 meant numerous targets in the lower route packs of North Vietnam, many of them of the "soft" variety. The Wing's aircraft began using 2.75-inch rocket pods as well as bombs and, when the defenses allowed, the Thuds would get "down in the weeds" to making strafing attacks on enemy troops, vehicles, and supply dumps to prevent any appreciable and dangerous buildup north of the DMZ. In June alone, the 388th expended no less than 150,000 rounds of 20mm ammunition during such strikes.

On 22 July, the Wing saw more changes of leadership when Paul Douglas handed over command to Colonel Allen K. McDonald. The two men would alternate as the 388th's commanders until the following June. McDonald was to pass the torch to Douglas on 18 August and take it up again on 15 December, thus giving Douglas the opportunity to run the show during the introduction to combat of the new F-4E Phantom during the late fall of 1968.

Other changes that would affect how the tactical fighter wings operated over SE Asia were also made at this time, when General John D. Ryan stepped down as PACAF chief. Into his shoes stepped General Joseph J. Nazzaro. Another ''bomber man'' from way back, Nazzaro nevertheless was reckoned to have a better grasp of the problems of tactical air combat than had his predecessor, and his willingness to overlook some of the more irksome rules and regulations made him a popular commander. In Vietnam, rules had a tendency to reach new heights of lunacy, and any man who showed flexibility in their application at the combat-unit level was very welcome indeed.

On a sadder note, General William W. Momyer relinquished command of 7th Air Force, the headquarters that had shouldered the responsibility of directing TAC fighter bomber operations since March 1966. In that time, Seventh had also taken more than a few brickbats, but throughout his two-year tenure, Momyer had proved capable of fielding most of them. While he misread the actions of the North Vietnamese Air Force on a couple of occasions and inevitably had to take unpopular decisions, Momyer's grasp of a highly charged combat scenario, probably unlike that any commander in history has had to face, was fundamentally sound. When he handed over his job to General George S. Brown, Momyer wrote an interesting dissertation on the performance of the US tactical air forces in the face of the MiG threat during Rolling Thunder.

In essence, Momyer stated that the USAF had been forced once again to reinvent the wheel as far as aerial combat went: the air war over North Vietnam had turned out to be very similar to other conflicts in that sophisticated weaponry's capability to destroy enemy fighters at long range was overridden by the need for visual confirmation, and thus the advantage invariably lay with the enemy rather than the attacking force. The USAF had few counters. Added to these drawbacks were the sanctuary areas handed to the NVNAF by the American rules of engagement. It was little wonder that the MiG kill ratio was barely above one-to-one. General Momyer was not alone in knowing what had gone wrong with the air war: it had never been fought along established, well-proven lines. By the time some moves were made to even up the odds, it was too late.

By August 1968, there were still three F-105 squadrons flying with the 388th and a similar number at Takhli. This provided a nominal strength of at least sixty-three aircraft on each base, a formidable force. But as the force was no longer needed to fly missions against the North, a degree of rationalization took place at this time. Squadron strength was reduced to eighteen aircraft each from the previous twenty-one, and some older F-105s, particularly long-serving D models, were returned to the US. An indication of how much combat time some of the Thailand-based Thuds had already put in was provided during the month by 60-0428 "Tiger" of the 388th, which had, in five hundred sorties, put in 3,000 flying hours. It was the first Thud to reach this impressive mark, although it was by no means the last.

In fact, the days of the single-seat F-105 in SE Asia were numbered. Even with the advent of the F-4 in the Wild Weasel role, the two-seat F-model Thud had plenty of work ahead. And in August, Republic flew the final F-105 model. This was the F-105G, the dedicated Weasel variant that carried the necessary radar sensors in two conformal fuselage pallets.

In the meantime, plans were made to convert two of the 388th's F-105 squadrons, the 34th and 469th, to the Phantom, with the 44th TFS remaining as the Korat-based Weasel unit. It was with some anticipation that the news of the long-nose F-4's impending combat debut was greeted, for this was, finally, a model with a built-in gun. The trouble was, there appeared to be little likelihood that the F-4E would ever be bloodied in aerial combat with MiGs—at least not in this war—and the crews who knew they had one of the most potent of the F-4 series had to be content with studying the manual on ground-attack techniques. It was what most of the fighting in Vietnam was about; killing MiGs never had a very high priority in the overall scheme of things—not officially, at least.

By September 1968, the 388th was able to announce that one of the Wing's pilots, Captain Peter K. Foley of the 469th TFS, had become only the third man in the Air Force to complete 200 missions.

The 388th had also had a hand in the first such cele-bration: that honor went to Major Larry D. Waller, who flew a hundred with Takhli's 34th TFS and a second hundred as a Weasel pilot with the 13th TFS out of Korat. Sadly, the second two-hundred-mission pilot, Lieutenant

Karl W. Richter, died of wounds shortly after reaching his double-century mark. Richter was rescued after being shot down, but his life could not be saved.

As one of the longest-serving TAC squadrons in Southeast Asia, the 469th continued to set records. In October, it passed the 40,000-combat-hours mark. By then, three F-105s had logged 3,000 hours.

Early in October, the strike wings carried out the heaviest attacks on North Vietnamese targets since July, when they put up a "maximum effort" against road transportation and vehicular traffic above the DMZ. Militarily, such destruction had only short-term effect; politically, it was felt at that time that it might do more harm than good. Peace talks had been taking place for some months, and although they were little more than talks about talks, the US presidential elections were imminent. With Johnson having announced that he would not seek renomination, he decided to terminate all action against any part of North Vietnam as a last act before leaving office. Thus, on 30 October 1968, Rolling Thunder ceased after three years and seven months.

Although the campaign was widely reckoned not to have achieved what the politicians had desired for it, the military men who had planned and executed the missions—from South Vietnam, from Thailand, from the decks of carriers out in the Gulf of Tonkin, and from as far away as Guam in the Marianas—had learned a great deal. Almost to a man, they had passed from a hypothetical, nuclear-war set of rules to a real-war situation that very few had ever envisaged happening after Korea.

The contingencies thrown up by Vietnam had necessitated new weapons and tactics to minimize casualties and, as far as was possible, carry out the job in hand. Given that the war very rapidly became all but unwinnable once the pattern of restrictions, delays, and downright confusion was set, little blame for the failure to force the required enemy capitulation could be laid at the door of the US Air Force, Navy or Marines.

In late 1968, very few knew what lay ahead. The end of Rolling Thunder turned out to be but a pause, albeit a long one, for one of the key elements of warfare employed by the United States.

9

I T was perhaps more than fitting that an outfit with a record as outstanding as that of the 469th TFS should have been chosen to introduce to combat what was undoubtedly the most potent model of the F-4 Phantom series. Incorporating a good deal of know-how accumulated by Air Force C and D models, the new F-4E not only looked different from all other models, it handled differently, had new systems, carried more fuel, and introduced integral gun armament. Tucked under a long, drooping snout, the gun was what Air Force pilots had always wanted on the F-4, as they believed that it could have made the difference in a number of tussles with MiGs. Once its missiles had been expended, the early F-4s were defenseless. Gun pods had alleviated the problem to some extent on the F-4D, but a gun slung under the fuselage or wing was not in the same class as a built-in weapon when it came to sighting.

Little wonder, then, that the young Turks who made up the squadron destined to be the first F-4E in SE Asia were itching to try their prowess and that of their new steed in the only combat scenario that meant very much to them—MiG hunting. But by the time the new F-4 was ready to make its bow, North Vietnam was off limits. Instead, crews learned how effective the F-4E could be in the ground-support role; there was still plenty of action to be had there.

Crews who would see that action were grouped into the 40th TFS of the 33rd TFW at Eglin AFB, Florida. This unit had been training Phantom crews since December 1966, and by 1968 was dispatching entire units to the war zone. On arrival, the 40th TFS lost its identity and the squadron took over the number of an existing unit within the wing—in this case, the 388th's 469th TFS. By flying over everything the squadron needed— aircraft, flight crews, maintenance echelons, and technicians—the 33rd Wing could reduce in-theater training to a minimum.

The reconstituted 469th was commanded by Lieutenant Colonel Edward Hillding. He had Tom McInerney as his weapons officer, and his task included instructing crews how to use the Bullpup air-to-ground missile. This weapon, among others, was intensely disliked by the airmen who were obliged to use it. It proved highly ineffective against targets such as bridges, and stories of how Bullpups bounced off such structures early in the Vietnam War hardly endeared it to the troops. High command eventually got the message and withdrew all Bullpups from inventory before the war ended.

The 40th TFS departed Eglin in some style. Several

members of the TAC top brass turned out to see the spectacle of sixteen F-4s blasting off, complete with garish sharkmouths adorning each one. Although the time-honored marking had given a touch of esprit de corps to combat aircraft since World War I, a ridiculous fuss was made about these particular "battle molars." Even in a war where commanders regularly sent out planes to incinerate people with napalm and no end of other horrendous weaponry, rude words or "aggressive" markings such as shark's teeth were verboten, at least on the aircraft that bore the bombs.

The force flew from Eglin-Hickam AFB, Hawaii-Andersen AB, Guam, and finally Korat, flight refueled en route. The transfer was made under the code name Operation 47 Buck 9, and all aircraft touched down safely at Korat on 17 November. On the 26th, the squadron fired up its new mounts and headed for Laos on the first F-4E combat mission of the war.

The bleating from the base weenies about those nasty shark's teeth was largely disregarded, although Hillding did issue orders that the aircraft be repainted when time permitted. In a combat zone, that could mean a long wait, and there were all sorts of legitimate-sounding delaying tactics to circumvent an unpopular order. Strength was added to crews' point of view when the incumbent Wing CO had one of the F-4Es painted with his personal insignia, teeth and all. Paul Douglas, or "P.P" as he was known, dubbed his aircraft "Arkansas Traveler II" and added his row of swastika kills to boot.

Not to be outdone in the paintwork stakes, Allen McDonald named his ship "Betty Lou." In common with other machines flown regularly by the same pilot,

McDonald added his name to the front-seat canopy bar
and that of his regular WSO, Lieutenant Jack Fisher, to
the one behind.

Despite the long periods of stand-down due to weather
and the general lack of missions with anything approaching a worthwhile target, the crews of the 469th showed
their mettle by painting many large, highly visible names
and cartoons on the flanks of their F-4Es, which were
distinctly flamboyant in comparison to even the recent
Thud days, when the markings had been distinctly sub-
dued. To the observer, all this might not have meant
much, but to the men at Korat it was an indication that
the war and the aircrews fighting it had changed. There
was perhaps a feeling that whatever the job, the Air Force
crews were now better equipped to do it, and do it well.
But any individual fighter pilot would have preferred to
take on all the MiGs in North Vietnam rather than haul
bombs to drop onto tiny targets all but hidden by the
endless canopy of jungle trees. But that, for the time
being, remained the nature of the task.

Nor was the burning issue of the shark's teeth over.
Before the 469th's aircraft had left the US, General Momyer had seen them and had not been pleased. A similar
negative impression was made on Lieutenant General
Edmundson, the PACAF vice commander, when he
stopped over at Korat in December. He ordered the teeth
off the aircraft, pronto. No matter if the 469th was then
turning in some of the best Bomb Damage Assessments
(BDAs) in SE Asia and morale was sky-high, the re-
painting had to be done. The issue was finally settled,
more or less, by PACAF chief General Nazzaro. Whether
or not the general had in mind how much his men had

owed to fighter pilots when he commanded a B-17 outfit in World War II is not on record, but the upshot of a conversation he had with Hillding was that he was more than prepared to look the other way if the 469th's aircraft continued to have teeth. They did.

The depletion of the F-105 inventory gave some urgency to equipping a second squadron of the 388th Wing with the F-4E, and even as the 469th began flying its first missions, aircraft and crews were being readied for the 34th TFS. But it would not be before the spring of 1969 that the unit finally bid farewell to the faithful Thud, and in the meantime, operations continued with it, albeit at a relatively low rate. The overall sortie rate for the years between Rolling Thunder and the actions initiated by Richard Nixon was to drop dramatically from the required effort during ''Johnson's war.''

Seventh Air Force Commander General George Brown was more than anxious to have the 388th become an all-F-4 Wing as soon as practicable, and while that plan pushed ahead, the erstwhile F-105 squadrons underwent some changes. The emphasis was now firmly on the Weasel mission despite the fact that fewer targets now required their specialized attention. Increasingly, the Thunderchief model to be seen in the blast-proof pens at Korat were the new G models, fully equipped to use the mighty Standard ARM.

The F-105G was the end result of a major industry program to keep the Weasel crews abreast of any electronic improvements the Russians incorporated into the equipment they supplied to North Vietnam. To a great extent, the USAF achieved this aim, particularly when the bombing halt curtailed Weasel missions. The combat debut of the Weasel Phantom lay some time in the future, and until the war heated up again the Thud crews honed their demanding art to an even finer edge.

With the inauguration of Richard Nixon on 20 January 1969, the changes brought about by events following the 1968 Tet Offensive in South Vietnam were, as far as the airmen in Thailand were concerned, ongoing. Pledged to bring the war to a satisfactory conclusion, Nixon inherited a very different kind of war from the one that had confronted Lyndon Johnson when he was catapulted onto the world stage in 1963. Initially, little happened; LBJ's bombing halt was still in effect, although Nixon was well aware of what the North Vietnamese were achieving without interference from US airpower. The new man in the White House did at least appreciate that in this he held a powerful trump card, which he had every intention of using if the US did not wrest a satisfactory cease-fire from the wreckage of the Paris peace talks—and soon.

Nixon's policy of ''Vietnamization'' of the war enabled him to initiate the gradual withdrawal of US ground forces without seeming to abandon the South Vietnamese to a forced unification of Vietnam. The US could hardly do otherwise, international pledges being what they were in those days, although the exponents of the old ''domino theory'' were not heard so much. Many individual Americans wanted out at any price.

Still playing by US rules, Nixon bided his time. His fear that the North was stockpiling munitions for a possible thrust across the DMZ was not without substance, as the continuing overflights of the areas now immune from attack brought back ample evidence of feverish activity. The road net named after North Vietnam's leader bulged at the seams with the amount of traffic it carried, even in the face of a rain of fire from the skies.

In Thailand, there had been a significant slimming down of Air Force units, but a leaner core structure remained. All five bases used by the Air Force remained open for business, and the Navy still deployed its carriers on Yankee Station.

Korat was a busy base by any standards, housing as it did units of the Royal Thai Air Force throughout the USAF's tenure. Among the older American aircraft that shared the base facilities were North American T-6 trainers and Bell UH-1 Huey helicopters. Even the lighter fixed-wing aircraft added to the pounding the Korat runway took, and in January 1969, the bulk of the 388th departed for a TDY spell at the neighboring F-4 base at Ubon while essential runway repairs were undertaken.

The North Vietnamese units infiltrating southern areas were not, of course, merely moving men and materiel and hiding from US air strikes en route and representing a largely passive force. On the contrary, the enemy spread antiaircraft defenses wide and deep so that while the heavier-caliber AAA and SAMs were not so much of a threat over Laos, through which long sections of the trail passed, lighter flak and small-arms fire represented a considerable hazard. Also, fighter Wings such as the 388th knew they could do little about the noise of their aircraft, which if anything, came to be more of a problem with the F-4 than with other types. The Phantom was also an unhealthy "smoker." The twin J79s belched out burned JP4 fumes to such an extent that the approach of an F-4 strike could be seen for miles, allowing the personnel and trucks that plied the Trail to all but disappear into the surrounding jungle.

Trail interdiction became more the province of slower, quieter aircraft, particularly toward the end of US involvement. But the jets were used when their heavy ordnance was believed to be the best to deal with given targets such as truck parks, supply dumps, and, frequently, the flak guns themselves. A Laotian target claimed the first of four F-4Es the 388th would lose in 1969 when the 469th's 67-0286 went down on 25 January.

But there is little doubt that the F-4E brought to Thailand a fearsome reputation for ordnance delivery, better even than previous Phantom models. And of course, if the target needed working over with 20mm fire, the Echo Phantom could do the job better than before. With its maximum five stores stations, four under the wings and one along the fuselage centerline, the F-4E could haul up to fourteen types of GP bomb, eight fire bombs, four folding-fin aircraft rocket launchers, and six different types of missile, not to mention the two types of gun pod then in use in the theater. The aircraft was also capable of carrying a range of flare dispensers and six different ECM pods as well as the standard external fuel tanks that comprised a pair holding 370 gallons apiece on the outboard wing stations and a 600-gallon tank on the centerline.

The close proximity of Laos to Thailand meant that the Air Force fighter bombers rarely needed to carry the maximum external fuel load, thus leaving all the wing racks free for the carriage of munitions, most of which could be loaded in multiples on ejector racks. This meant that just one F-4 could pack a heavyweight punch. Double or quadruple the number of aircraft increased the firepower accordingly, and just one flight of Phantoms could cause incredible damage to virtually any type of target.

Many missions flown by the 388th and other Wings were to deliver the highly effective cluster bombs. Devastating when dropped on any concentration of ground troops, particularly gun crews, cluster bombs came in no fewer than thirty-one varieties.

For tougher targets, the F-4 was modified to drop the remarkable series of optical- and laser-guided bombs. There were seven main types, with weights ranging from 560 lb for the M82 LGB to the massive 3,450 lb M118, which was optically guided via a miniature TV camera built into its nose. Never before had such capability been packed into one airframe, and it was little wonder that TAC commanders wanted as many F-4Es as possible on hand to meet any combat situation. Type commonality also assisted servicing and spares supply.

Throughout the lengthy period when the US was not conducting air strikes on North Vietnam, reconnaissance flights continued. Some of these were challenged, not always by ground fire. It was also frequently noted by Weasel aircraft that the enemy was tracking overflights on radar. The Americans believed this was a legitimate act of war, and there began a series of ''protective reaction'' sorties that resulted in ordnance being expended. Primarily such flights were in the nature of escort work, designed to protect recon planes if they were fired on or tracked: nobody could be sure that merely following a US photographic aircraft meant that the North Vietnamese were "handing it on" to be dealt with by defenses deeper in the country. The number of "incidents" began to climb.

By May 1969, the 34th TFS was winding down its F-105 operation at Korat in preparation for converting to Phantoms. The unit just missed being the second F-4E squadron in the theater, for in April the 4th TFS arrived at Da Nang. The 34th flew its final Thud sorties on 9 May and stood down. Less than one week later, on the 15th, it was able to fly its first F-4E sorties.

Among the 34th's ground crews who tended the various squadron aircraft at that time, and who usually had their names painted on the starboard side canopy bars, were the staff sergeants and sergeants, plus the airmen of various grades, all of whom kept their charges on the top line to meet mission requirements. Often unknown to the outside world, it is pleasing to record here a few of the people without whom the 388th and other combat Wings could hardly have functioned. An individual ground crew's association with a particular aircraft tended to last longer than that of the aircrew, for although aircraft were assigned to aircraft commanders and weapons systems operators/navigators, they were often flown on missions by other crews. But unless the aircraft was badly damaged and in the repair shops for any length of time, or was written off either in combat or as the result of an accident, the same ground crews would look after it for most of the time.

Thus, at Korat in the summer of 1969, a number of names were recorded, usually by ground personnel who took an interest in aircraft markings and color schemes. One such was David Hansen, who was part of the 388th

Field Maintenance Squadron throughout most of 1969. He noted not only the details of some 34th TFS aircraft on the base at that time, but also the people who flew and crewed the sharkmouth Phantoms. The full serial numbers of the following aircraft are listed in an appendix to this volume, and only the aircraft names are used here for brevity.

The earliest F-4E recorded in detail was "Sweetie Pie," on 17 July. Flown by Major Lem Jones and Captain Duane Tway, this ship was the responsibility of Staff Sergeants F. Reynolds and R. Hawkins. Three days later, Hansen's notebook recorded that "Okie," flown by Major Bill Whitten and Lieutenant Rhee Smith, was crewed by Staff Sergeant Kit Bucy and Sergeant Henry Smith. This particular F-4E, a Block 34 example off the McDonnell Douglas production line, became the 388th's second combat loss of the year.

On 24 July, Lieutenant Colonel T. G. Miller and Lieutenant R. A. Fisher crewed "Diane," with ground support in the hands of Staff Sergeant Campbell and Sergeant Schminkey. Two aircraft recorded on 26 August were "Spunky VI," flown by the future 388th wing commander, Colonel James M. Breedlove, back-seater Hawk Hawkinson, the charge of Airman First Class D. Hoffman and Sergeant L. Neely, and an unnamed Block 35 machine. This latter was the mount of Captain Don Irish (an appropriate green shamrock graced the portside air intake) and Lieutenant Doug Best. Sergeant T. Horton and A1C P. McCoy were the ground crew.

On 28 September, Major Don Parkhurst and Lieutenant "Black" Barton had their names painted on "Tiny Bubbles," alias F-4E 67-0279. Sergeant M. Linker was the only ground-crew name painted on at that date. This particular aircraft became the 388th's eighth Phantom loss, on 30 June 1970. Parkhurst and Barton then transferred to the "Wrecking Crew," which was crewed by Technical Sergeant Erskine and Staff Sergeant Maloney. Also on the flightline at Korat that day was "Li'l Buddha," with Major "Jack" Snyder as AC and Captain "Gus" Shackson occupying the rear seat. Staff Sergeant B. Rangel and Sergeant "Juan" Ochea kept this Block 36 F-4E in combat trim.

Finally in this brief survey, there was the oft-photographed "Here Come the Judge," which was looked after by Staff Sergeant Agee and Sergeant Sheldon when it was not being flown by Captain Dave Bean and Lieutenant Ed Ryan. It carried these names on 15 October. While the foregoing was a tiny part of the Korat scene during the early F-4E period, historians must be indebted to men such as David Hansen, particularly as combat aircraft change their colors frequently, either due to transfer to another unit, or by order of the brass. It was not too long before the 388th finally succumbed to edicts from above, and all this artwork, as well as those lovely teeth, disappeared.

Colonel McDonald ended his six-month tour as CO of the 388th on 10 June, his place being taken by John A. Nelson. The low number of combat operations continued at this time, and by year's end the 388th had lost another of its component squadrons when the famed 44th TFS Vampires transferred to Takhli.

War has been described as "ninety percent boredom, interrupted by short periods of sheer terror." Both came the way of many individuals at Korat during the years after Rolling Thunder, for although US troop withdrawals continued, there was no sign that the fighter bomber Wings would soon leave. Many men who finished their tours went home, and a lesser number of new crews came to start their own in the hot, humid atmosphere of Korat. Numerous training flights were made to initiate new guys to the unique operating conditions of Thailand.

There was also the terror. This accompanied most crews on the infrequent forays into Laos and Cambodia, for the Trail stayed open and the supplies kept rolling. The peace talks remained alive, although months went by without any great change in the agreements that had already been made by Nixon's negotiators. Not even the death of Ho Chi Minh on 4 September 1969 led, as might have been expected, to any new initiatives from North Vietnam. The US still maintained that South Vietnam should remain free to choose its own destiny and not have this dictated by Hanoi. In a positive move, the North had released the last of a third small batch of POWs in July. The stories these men told only confirmed US fears that their estwhile captors had hardly abided by the rules of war as enshrined in the Geneva Convention, and only full US withdrawal from SE Asia would see the rest finally freed.

10

I N common with thousands of other US servicemen, the commanders, flight personnel, and ground crews at Korat sweated out the years when there was little direct action against North Vietnam. A great many people wanted the thing to finally terminate so that they could go home, while others would have been pleased to have had one last crack at a job that was known to be unfinished. The US was caught on the horns of a dilemma: if peace was the main goal, it could not provoke any adverse reaction from Hanoi; on the other hand, protecting South Vietnam's interests had long meant hitting the enemy at source. Hanoi's view seemed to be that it had to bargain for peace with as much military strength as it could possibly muster, even if it meant unwittingly or deliberately sparking off US military action against what was seen as a violation of an uneasy truce. There were very few who had any idea which way the war was going to go, least of all the people who would have to do the fighting if it flared up again. Occasionally it did.

When US reconnaissance flights were fired on, Nixon authorized a series of protective reaction strikes. Launched only in direct retaliation to North Vietnamese military action, they gradually increased in number and scope. There were three types of protective reaction: (I) consisted of a small (one flight or less) force of fighter bombers providing close escort to reconnaissance flights; (II) were missions launched in support of US air operations in South Vietnam or Laos and there to "fire if fired upon"; and (III) was "reinforced" PR. These latter missions were carefully planned "surgical" air strikes in considerable force designed to take out selected targets on a "once only" basis. Target selection was authorized at the highest level in Washington, not locally. In general terms, all PR strikes were (perhaps somewhat optimistically) to be attacked once. No follow-up was planned, although it did happen that, say, a given radar site was attacked and only damaged. If that same site was on the air again at a later date—the rules of engagement interpreted enemy tracking of US aircraft by radar as a hostile act—it could legitimately be hit again.

Radar often made the difference between success and failure for both sides, and it was for this reason that the F-105G continued to play a vital part. Although all the Weasel ships remaining in Asia had gone to Takhli, Korat would again experience the roar of the mighty J75 engines—and soon. Some of the busiest aircraft in the theater, the Weasels flew missions anywhere that the North Vietnamese used radar; their expertise ensured that any mission had a better chance of success if the alerted enemy defenses knew the dangerous F-105s were up. It was often safer to shut down than stay "on the air" and risk destruction.

John Nelson handed over command of the 388th to Colonel James M. Breedlove on 5 December 1969. As related previously, Breedlove was no chairborne commander, and he continued to lead from the front seat of an F-4E when the paperwork permitted. A fourth Phantom was lost to the 388th's inventory the day the new CO took over.

Troop withdrawals saw a gradual drop in the number of US combat units in South Vietnam and an intensive training program to prepare the Vietnamese for whatever lay ahead. The Air Force expanded out of all recognition, and on the face of it, the South had ample ground and air assets to contain, if not beat, the forces ranged against it by the North. But even under war emergency conditions, the South Vietnamese could not hope to build the essential infrastructure to deploy armed forces with the required will and cohesiveness in such a short time scale. Under the circumstances, the US had little choice but to push the national takeover of war management as a viable proposition. The South Vietnamese government failed, perhaps, to realize just how much it relied on American support, particularly if it had been obliged to carry out air strikes on North Vietnam proper. While there was a widespread desire to do just that within the SVNAF, the Pentagon thought otherwise and denied the South any combat aircraft that would come near to surviving the North's defenses.

While Vietnamese ground-attack squadrons did achieve some impressive results with their AD Skyraiders, T-28s, and, later, jet types like the F-5 and A-37, they were restricted to a ground-support role largely within the borders of South Vietnam.

While the US strike squadrons remained in Thailand, the South had a powerful backup. These TAC aircraft, not to mention one of the most destructive heavy bomber forces in the world, namely SAC's B-52 fleet, were almost as dangerous to America's allies as to the enemy, in that when they were finally stood down, the South would find out just how naked and vulnerable it was. Far too heavy reliance on outside help was the fatal flaw in South Vietnam's struggle to remain independent. It was a gamble that might just have paid off before 1968; after that, it had very little chance as the American political and domestic lobby swung against South Vietnam and all it stood for.

It was perhaps surprising that USAF strike squadrons remained in SE Asia at all after the end of 1968, and it was due in great part to Richard Nixon's tough line that they stayed in place to make life difficult for forces bent on overthrow without popular election of government officials in line with democratic principles. Nixon at least believed that US military power could achieve the desired results if it was used correctly, but he was obliged to await overt action on the part of the North Vietnamese if this power was to be unleashed.

For the strike wings in Thailand, late 1970 saw more shifting around of units when it was decided to close Takhli. This base had been built almost from scratch when the USAF arrived to fly combat missions in 1965, and it was decided that Korat could handle the current decreased level of missions. Accordingly, Detachment I,

In typical early camouflage scheme that suppressed unit identity, F-105D 59-1749, alias 'Mr Toad/Marilee E' was part of the 469th TFS. (Republic)

A fully-laden Thud used most of Korat's 9,000 foot runway. An aircraft of the 34th is completing that exacting launch sequence in this view, armed with about the maximum iron bomb load. (Republic)

To take out SAM radars, Shrike missiles were useful, but the massive Standard ARM was preferred. This F-105F, 62-4434, tested the systems necessary to turn an F model into an F-105G, the majority of which had the QRC-380 electronic pallets along the lower fuselage sides. (USAF)

Phantoms and Thuds of the 388th formating on a KC-135 tanker during Linebacker operations. The nearest F-105G has the 17th WWS tail codes, two others those of the 561st and the F-4Es are from the 34th TFS. (Republic)

The F-4E came to Thailand with a fearsome reputation for ordnance delivery and only the enemy was disappointed. The 388th's sharkmouth marking caused consternation in higher echelons, but the Korat wing folks thought they looked just right. A prowling 469th TFS aircraft is seen here. (USAF)

Along the way, the 388th picked up the nickname 'The Wrecking Crew.' It was perpetuated on F-4E 67-0279 of the 34th TFS.

Another well-known and well decorated F-4E was 'Here Come the Judge,' seen here on a late war mission, when the final issue was no longer in doubt.

The Vought A-7D was a latecomer to the SEA war, but turned in a star performance. It was tough, fast and reliable and could carry a heavy load. This example is from the 355th TFW out of Davis Monthan AFB, Arizona. (Vought)

12th TFS, flew six aircraft plus personnel back to Korat in September. By year's end, these F-105Gs were the only Wild Weasel ships in the combat zone. They operated under the provisional designation 6010th Wild Weasel Squadron from 1 November. With the deactivation of the 388th's old rivals at Takhli on 10 December, five squadrons, including four that had borne the brunt of that base's F-105 effort during Rolling Thunder, were stood down. Included was the 44th, Korat's erstwhile Thud outfit. For TAC's air war against the North, it was truly the end of an era.

Korat and the 388th soldiered on, handling the missions as they came up. There was a big one fragged for 20 November, one that was destined to create big news. This was the daring but unsuccessful planned heist of US POWs from Son Tay Prison, situated twenty-eight miles from the center of Hanoi. Planned and executed in utmost secrecy, the C-130, HH-53, and HH-3 transport and helo force got into the prison compound while the Navy kept the attention of the North Vietnamese gunners in downtown Hanoi and the port of Haiphong.

With the loss of one helicopter, the raiding force inflicted a number of casualties and forced the enemy to fire off SAMs that failed to find any of the intended targets. This was surely due to the covering force of Korat F-105s, apparently included as a precaution at the last minute. Few people who planned the raid even knew that the Thuds were flying cover and acting as SAM bait while the Jolly Greens got clear.

Korat launched five F-105Gs as the Weasel decoy group, coded Firebird 1-5. The aircraft were flown respectively by: Lieutenant Colonel Robert J. Kronebusch and Major John Forrester; Major Raymond C. McAdoo and Major Robert J. Reisenwitz; Major Everett D. Fansler and Major William J. Starkey; Major Murray B. Denton and Captain Russell T. Ober; and Major Donald W. Kilgus and Captain Clarence T. Lowry. The last-named crew, of Firebird 5, were shot down, but fortunately both men were rescued.

The flight profile indicated for the Son Tay force Weasels was a lethal 13,000 feet, an ideal altitude for the enemy missile crews. Most of the SAMs were actually fired to detonate well above the F-105s, but there were one or two hairy moments. Firebird 3 dived to evade two SA-2s that were making straight for the Thud. Certain that both missiles were following, Major Starkey pulled up hard. He and Fansler watched one SA-2 arc overhead and explode behind the hurtling Thud, while the second dove underneath and expended itself in a fireball off the port wing. Fansler thought the explosion had set the wing on fire, but after about fifteen seconds, the fire went out and the F-105 continued to fly normally.

Less luck attended Firebird 5. A close SAM explosion lit up the cockpit like daylight, and Kilgus found he had lost stability augmentation control. It refused to re-engage, and Kilgus and Lowry knew the Thud, which was also leaking fuel, would not make it back to Korat. Over the Plaine de Jarres in southern Laos, the Thud flamed out at 32,000 feet. Gliding down to 8,000, Kilgus could not relight, and it was time to depart. Both men ejected.

En route home from Son Tay, the helicopters picked up the Weasel crews' bleepers, and at first light the choppers, covered by prowling Sandy A-1s, picked up Kilgus and Lowry, who had landed a half mile apart in the

Laotian jungle. Consequently, there were no American casualties on the abortive raid and, fortunately, no prisoners who could be forced to tell what they knew of the planning and execution. Don Kilgus was to receive fatal injuries later in the war.

The Son Tay force was launched from Korat when the 388th was under the command of Colonel Irby B. Jarvis, Jr. He had in turn replaced Colonel Ivan H. Dethman, the officer who had brought the F-111 to Thailand for its initial combat debut. "Ike" Dethman's tenure was short—less than one month, from 30 June to 29 July 1970.

At the end of 1970, Korat welcomed more Weasel crews to flesh out the 6010th, which had twelve aircraft by December. These machines were augmented by the EC-121s of the 553rd Reconnaissance Squadron, which began just over a year of operations from Korat starting 15 December. This "diversification" of units and aircraft types was by no means unusual at that time, and the established TAC fighter Wings increasingly became the reporting units for a wide range of aircraft with the specialized roles that the war had demanded. The 42nd Tactical Electronic Warfare Squadron brought its EB-66s into Korat on temporary assignment to the Wing for a period from mid-September to 14 October, the day before the unit was more or less permanently assigned until after the US involvement in combat operations.

The Weasels and ECM aircraft were based at Korat to support largely clandestine Air Force operations over Cambodia, ostensibly to deny areas of that country to the enemy as staging areas and supply routes into South Vietnam. These operations were conducted mainly by B-52s.

At the end of the year, there came the seemingly inevitable contribution to the war effort by the "number crunchers," that anonymous and probably significantly large army of troops whose lot it was to tally the credit/debit side of war. Vietnam was, if nothing else, a conflict of statistics. One that was gradually getting better was the F-105 loss rate for the previous twelve months. In 1970, this figure dropped to ten aircraft; while it did reflect the lower number of Thuds remaining on combat duty, it was a welcome one compared to the mortality rate of the 1960s. While not all the F-105s lost were from the 388th, the Wing had to record four F-4Es written off that year.

And before 1970 was out, there was a minor panic at Korat. Ryan was coming. Elevated from PACAF leader to USAF Chief of Staff, General Ryan was due to make a last visit to the combat units in Thailand. The word was that his inspection would extend to the flightline, where he was bound to see those garishly painted airplanes. Orders went out: repaint every aircraft on this base that has a sharkmouth, a name, or even command stripes. This time there was no ducking the issue. Paint and spray guns appeared as though by magic, and by working round the clock, the job was completed in time. The upshot to all this activity was that Ryan did not go near the flightline or even talk with anyone. Within a short time, the 388th's F-4s had their unit identity back.

Early 1971 was, like the previous two years or so, punctuated by short-duration missions, either of the protective reaction variety or to support equally brief drives against enemy buildup in Laos and Cambodia. Usually these missions were in support of other friendly forces, but on occasion, the Air Force alone handled the missions. Among these latter were Operation Louisville Slugger and Fracture Cross Alpha, in February and March, respectively. The first was a mere sixty-seven sorties against SAM sites in the Ban Korai pass area, and resulted in the destruction of a number of mobile SAM transporters.

Alpha was a series of PR strikes during 21–22 March, in conjunction with sorties by the Navy. Otherwise, 1971 was one of the least busy years for the USAF strike wings in Thailand: the 388th, for example, lost just three aircraft during the period, two F-4Es and a single F-105. There were incursions into the North and Laos, but such missions were carefully planned to minimize casualties and, indeed, were often unauthorized by Washington. It was later revealed that when General Lucius Clay, Jr., replaced Nazzaro as PACAF chief effective 1 August, his replacement at the head of Seventh Air Force had quietly directed strike forces to attack North Vietnam under his own Quick Check Recce plan. The instigator, General John D. Lavelle, was called to account for his actions, and he was eventually replaced prematurely by General John W. Vogt, Jr., in April 1972. Ironically, this was just as the fighting flared up again in the face of the North's spring invasion.

Before the end of 1971, the largest series of PR strikes yet gave some indication that the North might be flexing its muscles for something big. The buildup in the lower route packs above the DMZ was closely watched by US recon flights, and between 26–30 December Operation

Proud Deep Alpha took place. Striking areas south of the 20th parallel, Air Force and Navy aircraft flew 1,025 sorties, primarily against SAM sites and their radar guidance.

As peace talks continued and the South Vietnamese Air Force grew rapidly under now-urgent US reinforcement plans, the evidence of an impending enemy offensive gave cause for concern that the US could contain it. American troops were still going home under Nixon's policy, and the Air Force was still strong in the South. But if the enemy thrust was as large as was indicated and rumored, would the "backup," the Wings based in Thailand, be strong enough to mount another series of air strikes on the North?

11

PRIOR to 1972, the Korat-based Wild Weasel unit had undergone further changes. The provisional designation 6010th WWS lasted but two months, and on 12 January 1971 it had become the 17th WWS. At that time, the 44th and 354th Squadrons of the 355th were still functioning, but when these units were deactivated at the end of April, all Weasel assets were grouped under the command of the 17th.

Meantime, the all-Phantom 388th continued to operate as a two-squadron Wing (the 34th and 469th) with the 17th WWS making up the third squadron. In numerical terms, this meant that Korat supported thirty-five F-4s and sixteen F-105s. Other F-4 units were based at Ubon, Udorn, and Nakhon Phanom, as well as Da Nang—a total of 221 F-4s out of a total of some 800 US aircraft in Thailand and South Vietnam, plus nearly 1,300 SVNAF machines.

Before the 1972 spring invasion of the South, the 388th
had undergone more command changes. Colonel Irby
Jarvis handed over to Colonel Webb Thompson in July
1971, and Thompson in turn relinquished command to
Colonel Stanley M. Umstead on 14 December of that
year. Umstead would have the exacting task of accom-
modating additional strike squadrons at Korat and of directing operations during a very critical period.

As NVA troops assembled and tank commanders stud-
ied their maps for the big push, the North Vietnamese
Air Force was confident that it could give a good account
of itself if the Americans dared put in an appearance over
the homeland. The force was, as of March 1972, composed of 93 MiG-21s, 33 MiG-19s, and around 120 MiG-
17s and -15s. US intelligence estimated that around 190
NVNAF aircraft were serviceable and combat-ready at
that time.

The general breathing space between late 1968 and
early 1972 had given the North ample time to train and
deploy personnel tasked with operating the AAA and
SAM defenses. The guns and missiles had continued to
pour into the country during the false peace, and unlike
previous years, the enemy did not confine the larger-
caliber artillery pieces to the defense of major cities and
industrial centers—these had now spread right down
through North Vietnam to threaten overflights immediately above the DMZ. Courageous FAC pilots reported
guns and missile batteries in the hundreds, and if any
more evidence of Russian largesse in supplying SA-2s
was needed, one only had to count how many were fired
at even a small force of US aircraft. On 17 February

1971, for example, the enemy fired off 81 SAMs to bring down three F-4s in the DMZ area.

It was estimated that the air above North Vietnam was lethal up to nineteen miles high, and anyone flying into this lethal cone risked being brought down by any amount of gun or missile fire. The North Vietnamese rarely spared their SA-2s if they thought mass launches would destroy an enemy aircraft. The SA-2 could be fired either singly or in volleys of two or three, and as the war progressed through 1972 American pilots regularly observed barrage firing of dozens of SAMs at a time. Throughout the conflict, it was wl known that missile firings were out of all proportion to the number of aircraft they brought down. Accuracy often depended on the degree of harm Weasels and ECM jamming had been able to effect on the SAM's Fan Song radar; erratic "blind" launches were usually indicative of successful suppression tactics by the US aircrews, but the enemy rarely shied from trying for a lucky hit even when radars were down.

Ranged against this massive defense/offense force, the US made up in technical capability what it may have lacked in numbers, at least during the first three months of 1972, when "in-theater" assets were slim. As far as the strike wings were concerned—and this applied to virtually any aircraft obliged to run the gauntlet of NVA guns and missiles—the ongoing "fine-tuning" of the Wild Weasel mission had brought this particular form of protection to a high peak of efficiency.

With its updated radar homing and warning system, the F-105G was able to detect and track enemy radars on a wide band of differing frequencies. The main antiradar missile, the Standard, was also updated to incorporate an all-band seeker head, whereas earlier models had required two separate seekers. In the AGM-78B-2 and subsequent versions, the Weasel crews had a weapon able not only to destroy the target radar but also to mark their passage by different-colored smoke, thus making poststrike assessment easier. The F-105G was also equipped with a range of jamming devices that helped to nullify the numerical superiority the NVA enjoyed in this area: there were, of course, far more enemy radars than there ever were Wild Weasel aircraft to deploy against them. Rarely had the old adage "make every shot count" been more necessary.

Unlike iron bombs, the huge Standard ARM could be carried only singly or in pairs on each F-105. The more normal ordnance load was one Standard, two of the less effective Shrike ARMs, and a fuel tank occupying the remaining wing station. A long-range tank was invariably fitted on the fuselage station. Pilots would commonly use the wing-tank fuel on the early stages of the mission, just in case they had to jettison it in order to maneuver. Even so, the F-105G remained a heavy ship. This was emphasized in the summer of 1972, when crews launching from Korat found that the base's 9,000-foot strip of concrete ran out very quickly. After a number of Weasels were forced to abort because they simply could not get their heavy aircraft off in the distance, the problem was solved by leaving the bomb bay fuel tanks empty. Immediately after takeoff, tankers would refuel the Thuds.

SAC's tanker force was the lifeline of the tactical fighter bomber force in Thailand. Each F-105 and F-4 burned fuel at such a rate during maximum power maneuvers necessitated by the bristling defenses that it would have been near-impossible to sustain any kind of offensive without the "flying gas stations." And on numerous occasions the sight of a slowly orbiting KC-135 was the most welcome in the world to an exhausted fighter jock who had completed the mission and, perhaps, taken hits. Fuel leaks from punctured tanks or feed lines were not fatal if the tanks could be topped off faster than the gas ran out. By hitting a tanker before all the JP4 dripped away, a pilot had more than an even chance of making it back to base even though his ship was a flying wreck. Right from the start of USAF operations in SE Asia, the tanker force became an integral part of most strike missions into the North. SAC's Young Tigers, as the KC-135 force was dubbed, also inestimably aided the Air Force deployment of new or replacement units to the theater by offering a refueling service all the way from the States to the war zone.

As the new year 1972 dawned, it seemed probable that the North Vietnamese might open a new offensive during the Tet New Year holiday, just as they had in 1968. This did not materialize, and the next likely time was a few months hence, when Richard Nixon planned to become the first US president to visit the People's Republic of China. The early months of the year saw a number of US contingency plans swing into action to build up Air Force assets in SE Asia, ready for any eventuality.

The move of tactical aircraft from the US was under the code name Constant Guard, but in the event only SAC managed to complete the first phase of a new buildup in the western Pacific before the enemy struck.

In February, additional B-52s and their attendant KC-135 tankers were in place in anticipation of a new series of Arc Light bomber sorties. This operation, Bullet Shot I, was complete by the time Arc Light sorties restarted on 16 February.

In the early hours of Good Friday, 30 March 1972, the North Vietnamese struck. Opening their offensive with a massive artillery and mortar barrage, they soon had the South Vietnamese reeling and falling back. The invaders were helped by low cloud ceilings and dense overcast, which persisted for several days, preventing air attacks. All was confusion for a time, as cohesive reports of enemy gains were hard to obtain. It soon became clear, however, that the North was for the first time bent on a conventional thrust into the South with three divisions—about 40,000 troops. In support were not only tanks such as the T-54, T-34, and PT-76, but mobile guns and rocket launchers, including the SA-7 system and Russian 130mm guns, which had a firing range of up to seventeen miles. Nothing like this had ever been seen before on the battlefields of South Vietnam. The Communists' advance was rapid; sweeping through areas poorly defended by South Vietnamese marines and local "regional" and "popular" forces, they had thrust deep into Military Region I while a second, smaller force threatened Dak To airfield. A third North Vietnamese offensive was concurrently launched from Cambodia into northern Tay Ninh province.

The North Vietnamese apparently gambled on little or no US response to their actions, even believing that their mere presence in the South would have much the same shock impact as had the 1968 Tet Offensive. They also judged that the antiwar factions in the US would some-how prevent American military action on any scale and that any new battlefield casualties would bring the down-fall of Nixon. To their cost, the enemy totally misjudged the situation.

When the weather allowed, the Air Force and Navy mounted a number of ground-attack sorties against the invaders. Target identification remained difficult, and much reliance was placed on the FAC to mark, identify, and call in air strikes where they were most needed. The enemy had long realized the danger posed by the slow-moving FAC. Perched in a vulnerable O-1 Bird Dog or, later, a tougher O-2 or OV-10, the FAC possessed a terrible power. The enemy knew they could blow any number of these tiny planes out of the sky, but they could not be sure that the FAC would not be able to radio the necessary coordinates before he was forced off the air. If he did, more North Vietnamese would surely become casualties as the fighter bomber homed in.

The US gunship force, equipped with a variety of night-vision devices plus batteries of guns of all calibers, could keep up the pressure during the hours of darkness. And while the AC-119s and AC-130s were ostensibly vulnerable to ground fire, they did not usually venture over hot spots alone. Specialized night-flying Phantoms and F-105s could be called upon to keep the defenses busy while the transports worked over whole areas with their devastating rain of fire.

A key element in the US arsenal was the B-52. Used in a tactical bombing role, the giant eight-engined bomb-ers could be devastating. Often accused of dumping their huge loads of iron bombs on trees, the SAC bomber force remained the one element in the American inventory of combat weapons that the North could do little about over the battlefield. Although they were later to exact a toll of B-52s over North Vietnam, the enemy was all but naked to these high-altitude bomb swaths during the spring invasion.

Constant Guard I swung into action on 1 April. As soon as the invasion was recognized as the real thing, the migration of fighter bombers began. All Thai and South Vietnamese bases were slated for reinforcement, as the enemy showed little sign of being held by forces already in the theater. Aircraft bearing Air Force, Marine, and Navy markings were hurriedly armed and fueled for the trip across the Pacific either under their own power or on the decks of carriers.

Significantly, the first aircraft to depart the US were the F-105Gs of the 561st TFS at McConnell AFB, Kansas. These Weasels were urgently needed to handle the high threat posed by NVA missile batteries both inside North Vietnam and accompanying the invasion forces. The 561st left on 7 April and was in place at Korat by the 12th. Later that day, Weasel crews flew their first mission of this phase of the war. In support of the antiradar effort were six EB-66s configured as ''stand-off jammers.'' The F-105s and converted Destroyers were tasked more with the impending resumption of air strikes on North Vietnam proper than containing the enemy on the ground, and on 9 April, Freedom Train began where Rolling Thunder had left off.

There was considerable anticipation by the fighter pilots ordered to move to SE Asia that the NVNAF would offer them the chance of further MiG kills. For its turn, the front-line MiG force was ready to take on the Americans once more. Those pilots who had come through the 1960s air combat rounds now had more and better aircraft, although a few preferred to stick with the obsolete yet highly maneuverable MiG-17 rather than use the MiG-21. New to combat since the Americans last appeared over North Vietnam in force was the MiG-19. This excellent dogfighter offered the safety margin of two engines, supersonic performance, and a heavy armament comprising both cannon and AAMs.

The first MiG to be shot down during the period was claimed by an F-4D of the 3rd TFW on 30 March. It was the third MiG credited to Air Force flyers in 1972. At Korat, as at other bases, the men of the 388th noted these successes with interest but wished that it had been their own unit that had taken the credit. It was to be a few weeks yet before the Korat Wing would score again, and the pilots were chagrined to note that it was a crew from the 366th TFW that made the first kill with the F-4E. And the competition was mounting; although the 388th had been the first to fly the gun Phantom in combat, it was now far from unique in that respect. Everyone vowed that the TDY squadrons from the States would not take all the glory away from the "old heads."

To feed more airpower into critical points in the South, TAC established, on 15 April, turnaround facilities at Bien Hoa to support air strikes in Military Region II. Refueling and re-arming closer to the battlefront meant more TOT—time on target—and more ordnance. Over North Vietnam that same day, an F-105G of the 17th WWS was shot down and the crew taken prisoner.

The battle for the South raged through the summer

months as the US and SVNAF poured fire onto the advancing enemy. But the sheer weight of the forces involved, their initial momentum under the bad-weather respite enjoyed in the earliest days, and their own massive defensive firepower, ensured that the task of stopping them was far from easy. Ground was lost at numerous points, and on 24 April, Dak To airfield had to be abandoned.

In the meantime, Air Force and Navy strikes were mounted against some old targets in grimly remembered hunting grounds up north. In particular, the bridges that had defied so many iron bombs were sought out. In 1972, weapons development enabled a very small force, carrying its own protection in the form of chaff and ECM pods, to go in and attack with stand-off bombs. The infamous Thanh Hoa ("Dragon's Jaw") was attacked by F-4s of the 8th TFW. But this crudely built, highly resilient structure was to defy technology for a little longer yet: the same Wing all but wrecked it in a second attack on 13 May, but there were in fact to be another thirteen strikes before the Dragon was deemed to have expired.

The Vietnamese delegation walked out of the peace talks on 4 May, and further talks were canceled for the immediate future. Hanoi still showed little inclination to comply with Nixon's demands for a reasonable settlement. Air strikes on the North were stepped up, and on 8 May Linebacker I began with mining sorties off Haiphong. Intended as a short, violent reminder of what US airpower could do if the North did not make positive moves to end the war, Linebacker I was primarily handled by the Air Force and Navy flying an intense series of tactical sorties. It was to bring out the NVNAF in force and lead to losses for both sides.

Two days into Linebacker, 10 May 1972, recorded the greatest victory over the enemy MiG force—eleven shot down by Air Force and Navy pilots. As the Air Force went after bridges and other targets, MiGs and Phantoms tussled. Both sides lost people who were considered to be among the best pilots: Lieutenant Randy Cunningham and Lieutenant (Jg) Willie Driscoll dispatched the MiG-17 flown by the mysterious "Colonel Tomb" to make them aces, and a pilot named Guen Doc of the North Vietnamese AF's 3rd Company shot down two F-4s in his MiG-19, one of them Major Robert Lodge and his navigator, Captain Roger Locher, of the 432nd TRW.

The 388th fielded a strong force of fifteen Weasels to cover the forces out to nail more bridges, including the Paul Doumer. Four EB-66s added their ECM capability, and the laser and electro-optical bombs did severe damage. Follow-up strikes had put the bridge out of commission by the 13th. Two days before, another two men were introduced to the doubtful hospitality of the Hanoi Hilton when a Weasel crew from the 17th were captured after their Thud was shot down.

By the end of May, the Air Force estimated that thirteen bridges had been put out of action. During Linebacker the main targets had been enemy lines of communication, but the battlefield now extended into South Vietnam. Attack sorties rose rapidly, and they soon reached an average of 15,000 per month, about two-thirds that of Rolling Thunder.

The bases in Thailand and Vietnam welcomed the

"summer help" by the TAC units that came into the war theater under Constant Guard I and II, the latter being the largest single overseas movement of forces in TAC's history. Among other requirements was the need to re-open Takhli as an operational base. The home of the 388th's rival Thud wing in the old days, Takhli had been placed on caretaker status under the Royal Thai Air Force for more than a year, but the new buildup meant that it was needed again, particularly to house elements of the SAC tanker force to support TAC operations while the crisis lasted.

Korat also got its tanker fleet when seven KC-135s and twelve crews arrived under the Tiger Claw deployment between 12 and 17 June. These tankers, assigned to the 4104th Air Refueling Squadron, Provisional, directly supported Korat's strike, ECM, and recon force, effective 9 June. The move was part of a SAC plan to provide tankers to meet all refueling requirements at tactical air bases on a day-to-day basis. In Korat's case, a minimum of six tanker sorties per day was initially established.

A sidelight to the assignment of tankers to Korat was that one of them suddenly sprouted shark's teeth. Such markings would have been frowned upon outside the combat zone, and only one other SAC aircraft, a B-52, is known to have had similar embellishment. Colonel Umstead and the men of the 388th were delighted. It literally marked the tanker as one of their own and looked just right alongside their F-4s.

Gradually, the spirited response to the NVA invasion brought results. The enemy faltered and then began to fall back under intense pressure from forces fighting hard on the ground, ably assisted by a solid wall of friendly airpower overhead. And this time, the air war saw few restrictions, particularly in attacks on the North; the US president, not to mention the electorate, was fed up with the time it was taking to wrap up the Vietnam War. Nixon wanted an end to the time-wasting by the North Vietnamese delegation to the Paris peace talks—time that was invariably turned to enemy advantage on the battlefields thousands of miles distant. Determined that his "peace with honor" pledge would still have some credence, Nixon knew that it now meant stopping the NVA in its tracks before the invasion consolidated a stranglehold on key areas of the South and strengthened the other side's peace-settlement conditions.

Such heady objectives probably did not occupy the thoughts of Aircraft Commander Lieutenant Colonel Von Christiansen, or those of his back-seater, Major Kaye Hardin, as they scanned the sky outside their F-4 cockpit on 21 June. The mission drawn by the 469th Squadron that day was to cover two flights of fighter bombers dropping chaff to confuse enemy radar coverage of targets in Route Pack VI.

Two MiG-21s then put in an appearance, one going after the chaff bombers and the other pursuing the lead F-4E in the 469th flight, Iceman O1, flown by Colonel Mele Vojvodich, Jr., and Major Robert M. Maltbie.

Rather than two enemy fighters, Vojvodich reported that he saw three. He fired a missile at one but could not observe the result as he was distracted by another MiG. When the results of the combat were known, it seemed

that Iceman O3 (Christiansen/Harden) had probably
saved Vojvodich by calling a break as one MiG homed
in on him.

Christiansen initially sighted the MiGs at twelve
o'clock high to the chaff flight, crossing their egress
course from left to right, some two to three thousand feet
above. The enemy fighters were using the cover provided
by a 500-foot-thick broken overcast, while the chaff force
was about 100 feet below the cloud layer.

Making a hard right turn as they came abreast of the
chaff force, the MiGs initiated an attack, but as they did
so the number-two enemy fighter appeared to spot Iceman
O1 and O2 below. Pulling up, this MiG started an attack,
probably failing to see the other two F-4s in the Iceman
flight. Christiansen called the break as the MiG fired two
AAMs at Iceman 2. The Phantom evaded the Atoll salvo
with a hard left turn.

The attacking MiG-21, in 'burner, was egressing the
combat area when Christiansen maneuvered in behind
him, five to six thousand feet behind. Acquiring a full
system lock-on, the American pilot tried to fire two AIM-
7s. Both Sparrows failed to launch. Christiansen then
obtained a strong IR Sidewinder tone and fired three as
the MiG hung in his gunsight reticle, gently banking
right. The AIM-9 ripple shot did the trick, although one
missile exploded about fifty feet off the MiG's tail. The
second Sidewinder got him. It was seen by Harden to
explode the MiG, which fell away, burning aft of the
canopy. The pilot ejected, and a yellow 'chute was seen.
Nobody saw what happened to the remaining AIM-9, as
Christiansen and Harden had to turn their attention to the

second MiG, now pulling off after attacking the chaff flight.

A max power pull-up and some maneuvering put the F-4E in the MiG's six o'clock. This MiG had led the flight, and the pilot knew his business. He tried everything to shake the pursuing F-4, throwing his fighter in a series of maneuvers that took him from 20,000 feet down to 1,000 feet. Still the American crew closed, intending to make a gun attack. Although radar lock-on was obtained, Christiansen doubted that his tracking was perfect. His first burst was fired from 3,000 feet separation, and he continued snapping out short-duration bursts as the range closed. Trying to correct a suspected gunsight lead prediction problem, the F-4 pilot aimed slightly ahead of his quarry. This seemed to improve things, and strikes were observed on the MiG's left wing just as the M-61 abruptly stopped firing, out of ammunition. Iceman O3 headed out with fuel at bingo state. One down and one damaged wasn't at all bad, and when the kill was confirmed the 388th Wing had its first victory since 23 August 1967.

12

THE June MiG victory for the 388th heralded further
success, but not before the fall of 1972. And there
was a price. Another F-4E had been lost on 8 June,
and other F-4 units had to record the fact that combat
with the NVNAF was not a one-sided affair. On 24 June,
eighteen-plus F-4s of the 8th and 366th Wings were tar-
geted against the Thai Nguyen steel works. Bounced by
Nguyen Duc Soat's 3rd Company of MiG-21s, the American formation lost two F-4Ds, one from each Wing.

The North Vietnamese ace was in action again on the
27th, claiming four F-4s downed. The US Department
of Defense made it only three, two from the 366th and
one from the 432nd TRW. After the war, the Air Force
and Navy minutely analyzed each air combat to find out
why the air-to-air kill ratio over the MiG force was so
close. It came out at slightly above two-to-one, the worst

ever the US had experienced. Little could be done to
improve things while the war was being waged, however.

In July, the 388th also lost aircraft to the MiGs, two
F-4Es going down on the 5th. Both aircraft were from
the 34th TFS, which had to add another aircraft lost on
the first day of the month during a sortie over the North.
Losing aircraft and crews to ground fire was one thing;
coming off second best to the much smaller MiG force
hurt too. On the face of it, the detection devices available
to the Americans should all but have prevented any surprise attack from materializing, and most strike sorties
were accompanied by MiGCAP F-4s that were along
specifically to fight MiGs. But then again, theory rarely
agreed with actual events; nearly always, the US crews
had other aircraft to protect and were not free (as the
enemy pilots were) to chase MiGs all over the sky, as
they had been, for example, in Korea. In Vietnam, the
initiative invariably lay with the defenders rather than the
attackers, and the favorite MiG tactic of hit-and-run still
paid off on occasion. Seeing the enemy aircraft on radar
or by the human eye was one thing, but preventing him
from getting a fatal shot at one or two of the multiple
targets he had to choose from was often very difficult,
if not impossible.

The Korat-based F-105G Weasels accompanied most
strikes into the North during both Linebacker phases.
Apart from those rare occasions when the planners reckoned there was a good chance that a small force of F-4s
alone could hit the target by surprising the defenses, the
Weasels carried on their war against NVA radars. But
there never were enough of them. One solution was
to free the Thuds from having to shoulder the whole

mission—detection and attack—in Flight strength or less. This was achieved by forming "hunter-killer" teams, whereby the F-105s were paired with F-4s, the latter carrying a heavy ordnance load to ensure that once the Weasel bird found a radar target, it stayed off the air for good. Having F-4 backup also meant that there was more chance of putting the enemy out of action permanently; if the limited missile armament of one or two F-105s should malfunction or simply miss, the following F-4s could usually pick up the slack.

The only exception to the need for any kind of support was the second series of strikes conducted by the F-111 during Linebacker. This time, the "Aardvark" performed amazingly well. Its systems were so advanced that one aircraft could brave the defenses with impunity, in total darkness, and strike a pinpoint target hard. Using the magic of terrain-following radar, the F-111 could fly and fight under conditions that would have been fatal to almost any other airplane. But again, the biggest drawback was that it was available in very small numbers.

In August the USAF, perhaps with some relief, announced that it had its first ace in Vietnam. Steve Ritchie's five kills to elevate him to this vaunted status came none too soon: the Air Force had been in SE Asia for nearly ten years by then, and in comparison with other wars, taking this long to confirm that one pilot had destroyed five of the enemy in combat was little short of amazing. This would, of course, totally overlook the chance for US pilots to rack up multiple kills and in this and many other respects, Vietnam has no comparison.

The last quarter of 1972 saw something of a crescendo as Linebacker strikes systematically struck many North

Vietnamese targets off the list. In the South, too, the ground forces had succeeded in holding territory, and there was every sign that the enemy offensive had been a costly gamble that failed. No matter how heavy fixed or mobile antiaircraft defense is, it is a military fact that to have no air cover courts disaster for tactical battlefield movement of tanks, vehicles, and troops. And the North never did have any air support for its ground forces.

Early September saw the start of another run of MiG kills for the hardworking crews of the 388th. On the 2nd, an F-4E, crewed by AC Major Jon I. Lucas and 1/Lt Douglas G. Malloy shot down a MiG-19. The crew mix in this particular Phantom was a little unusual, as each man was assigned to a different squadron. Major Lucas was a member of the 34th, while his WSO hailed from the 35th TFS, the unit that had been of TDY with the 388th since June. This welcome boosting of the Korat Wing's fighter force was to last until October, two weeks or so before Linebacker I was concluded.

The task that day was a hunter-killer sortie to Phuc Yen airfield, Eagle Flight comprising a pair of F-105Gs and two F-4Es. This element was seeking out SAM sites when a MiG-19 attacked one of the Thuds, call sign Eagle 02. The enemy pilot's opening gambit was an Atoll AAM that missed the F-105 by twenty feet. The crew, Major Thomas J. Coady and Major Harold E. Kurz, threw their aircraft into a hard right turn to avoid, whereupon the MiG driver bored in for a cannon attack on Eagle Lead, the second Thud. A hard right turn also saved this crew, Major Edward Y. Cleveland and Captain Michael B. O'Brien.

As the MiG broke off, it passed over the F-4E of Lucas

and Malloy, hightailing it east, inverted. The Americans reckoned the MiG was heading for Phuc Yen. The F-4 gave chase.

Malloy quickly set up the enemy fighter and confirmed bore-sight acquisition. He obtained lock-on, and Lucas "squeezed the trigger." The instrument panel indicated that the F-4's aft left side AIM-7 had launched.

Lucas armed the gun to follow through with 20mm fire, if necessary, but just then a SAM was seen, tracking the F-4. A turn into the missile to negate its track caused the crew to lose sight of the MiG and its demise by the Sparrow. The next thing seen was the pilot's orange parachute. Major Cleveland did see the missile impact the enemy fighter and watched it spiral down. The kill was confirmed.

This combat was but a prelude to the 388th's most successful day of the war in terms of MiG kills when the Wing scored a triple. The first day of combat, 12 September, saw the US pilots in a high state of confidence for three days beforehand. Major Charles DeBellevue had engineered the destruction of his fifth and sixth kills to make him the USAF's second ace and the leading MiG-killer of the war.

Two of the MiG-21s downed on 12 September fell to the same Flight of the 388th. Finch Flight was acting as escort to chaff flights heading northeast of Hanoi in the vicinity of Kep airfield when a group of MiG-21s attacked.

From four to six o'clock positions, the MiGs latched on to one of the chaff flights. Finch Lead, Lieutenant Colonel Lyle L. Beckers and 1/Lt Thomas M Griffin, saw one MiG lining up for a missile shot on the rear elements of the chaff flight. Beckers obtained an auto-acquisition lock-on and attempted to fire two Sparrows while the MiG-21 launched an Atoll at his target, broke away, and dived. Beckers and Griffin switched to Sidewinders and fired two. One was seen to impact the MiG's left wing, which emitted flames and smoke. Close enough for a gun attack, Beckers opened fire. He gave the MiG 520 rounds of HEI/tracer and more damage was inflicted. The F-4 broke off, the crew last seeing the MiG ascending steeply, on fire.

The MiG pilot's Atoll had, however, taken out one of the chaff bombers in the classic hit-and-run at which the NVNAF was so adept. While Beckers and Griffin had taken care of one MiG, Finch 03 (Major Gary L. Retterbush and 1/Lt Daniel L. Autrey) was dealing with another. Turning into the enemy fighter, Retterbush got a good radar lock-on. He fired two AIM-7s, which failed to guide (a not unusual occurrence). Retterbush had no better success with a follow-up ripple of three Sidewinders. All his missiles missed by what he judged was a matter of feet. Retterbush lined up on another MiG in the enemy flight and closed for a gun attack. This time, the enemy aircraft did not evade: the F-4's gun pumped out 350 rounds, which impacted all along the fuselage and punctured its wing. It went into an uncontrolled climb, slowed to 150 kts, and dropped. The F-4 crew reported seeing the pilot slumped over his controls, and as they egressed the area, observed a smoke trail and a large fireball.

Later the same day, Robin Flight of the 388th, comprising three F-4Es and an F-4D in the number-two slot, was covering a strike on the Tuan Quan railroad bridge when two MiG-21s attacked. One appeared from eight o'clock and lined up on the strike flight. Robin Lead fired an AIM-7 to get the MiG pilot's attention. It did. The missile exploded about 1,000 feet ahead of the Phantom, and the MiG broke away. Lead pursued and tried to nail him with another Sparrow and three Sidewinders. All missed.

A second MiG suddenly dropped down between two F-4s, according to the crew of Robin 02, Captain Michael J. Mahaffrey and 1/Lt George I. Shields. Mahaffrey rolled right, tracked the MiG, and fired a single AIM-9. Hit in the tail section, the MiG-21 began to shed parts. It went into a spin from 16,000 feet, with more bits breaking away. It never recovered. Last seen by the F-4 crew still spinning below 8,000 feet altitude, it apparently fell about twenty miles southwest of Yen Bai airfield. That made it three for the day.

As though to even up the score, the 388th lost another F-4E and two more F-105Gs before September was out. But early October saw the pendulum swing again in the Wing's favor. On the 5th, Captain Richard E. Coe and 1/Lt Omri K. Webb III faced a potentially dangerous situation by flying up north with just two aircraft in the flight. The other pair had been forced to abort the mission and the rules said you shouldn't go on a strike support with just two aircraft. Dick Coe pressed on anyway, as the second abort did not happen until Robin Flight was en route for the tanker rendezvous. Coe was in fact a spare flight lead that day, and he had filled the slot when the original leader was forced to bow out. Thus depleted, Robin 01 and 04 (Captains Dave Ladd and George Sebren) led the escort to two flights of bombers with Weasel support. Three MiGCAP flights were also on the mission, which was, like all others during this period, to Route Pack VI. F-4s with laser-guided bombs were briefed to attack points on the northeast rail line linking Hanoi with Red China.

The force flew out over the Gulf of Tonkin to come in from the east just below the Chinese border. This avoided overflying too much North Vietnamese territory and reduced the risk of losses to ground fire and SAMs. MiG activity was reported by Red Crown, the Navy's shipboard MiG watch, and then Air Force GCI, but other prowling F-4s quickly reduced this threat.

It was common for the enemy to use multiple radars to track US aircraft, the intention being to distract the aircrews from the sneak MiG attack. With their headsets full of warnings, the pilots and WSOs had to keep a good visual scan for just this type of attack, which often came from below as the MiGs kept in the dark, ground-return-saturated areas where the US radars could not detect them. Dick Coe's primary concern was the favored MiG stern attack from directly behind. "Watch your six" was foremost in the fighter pilot's creed. The first MiGs seen by Robin Flight were off to their right. Screaming along just below the Chinese border, Ken Webb called in two. Then there were another two, climbing out of the Hanoi area but still too low for the escort to pick them up. At that moment, the strike lead called that he was under attack from his six. Momentarily confused by this, Coe and Webb saw the strike lead jettison his ordnance and depart.

Then Coe saw two MiGs in front of him, about three miles away at about 20,000 feet. Doing Mach 1.6, the

shark-nosed Phantom rapidly overhauled the pair of
MiGs. But the enemy pilots were not hanging around as
Coe counted off the required seconds to let the AIM-7's
electronics settle. He fired one. Immediately a MiG call
came in: someone had a fighter on his tail. In that situation, you don't wait to find out who it is—you break.
Coe did just that, losing sight of his Sparrow. The next
thing he saw was a huge black explosion and two puffs
of white smoke.

Webb called another break, and the F-4 took an airframe load of 9 G. Two MiGs overshot. Reversing, Coe
and Webb tried to catch them, but they had disappeared.
A call from Robin 04 that his fuel was at "joker
state"—500 lb above bingo—made it time to go home.

Back at Korat, Coe and Webb were delighted to hear
that the two MiGs they had fired at had lost one to their
missile. It was confirmed by a MiGCAP flight high above
the action, so another MiG kill flag was hoisted over the
34th TFS compound at Korat as well as a red star being
applied to the F-4E Coe and Webb had flown that day,
serial number 68-0493.

The following day, 6 October, another MiG was to
fall to the 34th, this one having the unusual distinction
of being shared by two crews—or, as the Air Force
tended to share credit equally between aircraft commanders and back-seaters, a quarter share to four individuals. The manner in which the MiG was destroyed
was unusual. It might have been an indication of another
period, when the MiG force had to throw inexperienced
pilots into battle, following the recent losses in the air
and on the ground. On 1 October, heavy air strikes on
North Vietnam's airfields at Phuc Yen, Yen Bai, Vinh,

and Quang Lang had destroyed at least five enemy fighters and damaged nine others.

On 6 October, a 388th hunter-killer team was again using the call sign Eagle. The composite F-105G/F-4E flight had Major Gordon L. Clouser and 1/Lt Cecil H. Brunson in Eagle 03, with Captain Charles D. Barton and 1/Lt George D. Watson as number four. Disco warned of approaching MiGs when the flight was in the vicinity of Thai Nguyen, and as prebriefed, the two F-105s moved out of the area while the Phantoms took on the MiGs. Clouser and Brunson saw a MiG-21 at seven o'clock and, almost simultaneously, a MiG-19 coming in at six o'clock to their element. Calling a hard left break to divert the MiGs from the F-105s, Clouser jettisoned his ordnance and fuel tanks. Barton followed suit.

The MiGs were then very close to firing position. Clouser flung the Phantom into a dive, while Barton maneuvered to throw the MiG driver's aim. With both backseaters keeping tabs on the MiGs, they saw the '19 follow Barton, firing as he went. Clouser rolled in behind, sandwiching the MiG, whereupon the MiG-21 dived onto Clouser's tail. The quartet continued to dive until Barton bottomed out three-hundred feet above a valley floor between two mountains. The MiG-19 pilot apparently failed to notice the speed at which he was approaching the ground until it was too late. His frantic efforts to pull up failed, and he went in. Both F-4Es recovered, and the MiG-21 sheered off to offer no more of a challenge. Eagle 03 and 04 shared the fifteenth kill by the 388th to date.

Gary Retterbush got a second kill on 8 October. Teamed with Captain Robert H. Jasperson, he was Lark

Flight lead on a strike escort. MiG warnings were received, and Retterbush jettisoned tanks to maneuver. On the tail of a MiG-21 taking evasive action, Retterbush could not get his AIM-9s to fire, so he closed in for a gun shot. Several good hits were observed, and the MiG burst into flames. The pilot ejected at about 1,500 feet before the fighter hit the ground.

Three more MiGs fell to Air Force pilots before Major Robert L. Holz and 1/Lt William C. Diehl wrapped up the Korat Wing's MiG victory roll with a MiG-21 on 15 October. Flying as Parrot 3, Holz and Diehl were escorting three flights of F-4 strike bombers to Viet Tri. Three enemy fighters were downed that day, and there were numerous combats. Holz and Diehl engaged a number of MiG-21s; Red Crown vectored them onto two MiGs at their twelve o'clock position, these being visually observed about two miles away. Making a hard left turn, the F-4 crew saw these particular MiGs make a fast egress out of the combat area, no longer a threat to the strike force. Parrot 3's wingman then had an inconclusive shot at a MiG-21 before this one disappeared in cloud.

Finding themselves way behind the strike bombers, Holz and Diehl elected to orbit in the Viet Tri area and wait to cover the bombers on egress. While doing this, there was another "no result" skirmish before more F-4s separated Parrot flight, bent on another MiG kill.

Right turning to join his wingman, Holz noted a white 'chute three to four thousand feet above the ground and had his back-seater note the time and location in case it was an American who had hit the silk. Then Holz saw a MiG-21 ominously circling the parachute at the same altitude. In a lazy bank about 3,000 feet ahead of the

F-4, the MiG pilot appeared not to notice his pursuer—
until a Sidewinder went straight up his tailpipe. Pieces
of tail section and almost a complete elevator departed
the MiG airframe. It rolled violently to the right and
started down, on fire. Parrot 3 then departed. And that,
unknown to Holz and Diehl and the other crews of the
388th, was it.

Seven more MiGs were to fall up to 8 January 1973,
two of them being credited to B-52 gunners, but the 388th
was not among the victors. The Wing's score stood at a
very respectable seventeen for the war.

A sad note for the Wing in October was the loss of
another F-4E to the Vietnamese pilot Duc Soat. He
claimed a 469th aircraft on the 12th, two days after
the 35th TFS ended its TDY and departed Korat. But
the Wing was not to be depleted, for the month saw the
arrival of not only new squadrons but new aircraft, one
of which was new to both the Air Force and the war.
This was the Vought A-7, the USAF version of the Navy
Corsair II attack bomber, in the hands of the 354th TFW.
First unit to fly the type, the 354th sent an Advance
Echelon to Korat on 14 October on detachment to Seventh
Air Force. The unit commenced combat operations two
days later.

The other new type on the Korat flightline was, to a
casual observer, not new at all. What he would have seen
were twelve F-4C Phantoms, a familiar enough aircraft
in Thailand and South Vietnam. What was not so familiar
was the job these machines, belonging to the 67th TFS,
had been sent to do. These were the ''new generation''
of Wild Weasel, the result of a lengthy program of modification to enable the trusty F-4 to undertake the Weasel

mission. Chock-full of new radar homing devices and wired to use the Shrike ARM, these F-4s were stationed at Korat to prove that the Phantom could henceforth undertake this important task beyond the time when the last F-105 was retired. Regarded as interim models due to their inability to carry the Standard ARM, the Weasel F-4s nevertheless began to give a good account of themselves as Linebacker I entered its last days.

13

DESPITE a bout of bad weather through July and August, TAC sorties were launched against various targets in North Vietnam and the invasion forces south of the DMZ; gradually the combined weight of air and ground firepower began to break the back of the Easter offensive. On 24 July, LGBs were used on targets in the Hanoi area for the first time in a month. On 9 August, Kep airfield was bombed, the defenses being subject to a heavy rain of chaff to protect the strike force. Three days later, it was announced that the last US ground troops had been pulled out of South Vietnam.

The sortie rate reached a 1972 high on 16 August, when 370 were flown against northern targets in improving weather. Concurrently, 294 sorties were flown in the South. Toward the end of August, the Xom Bai barracks complex thirty-seven miles northwest of Hanoi was heavily hit, the air attacks destroying an estimated ninety-six buildings and damaging seventy-eight. The bombers also left their calling cards on Hai Dung barracks, twenty-three miles southwest of the North Vietnamese capital, and also attacked bridges on the northeast rail line.

With the ground war solely in the hands of South Vietnamese and Allied troops, the US, with some satisfaction, saw that its recent policy seemed to be working. After some initial setbacks the South rallied and fought well, exacting a terrible price in men and materiel from the invaders. The on-off peace talks remained stalled while the heavy fighting continued, but there were signs that the NVA was far from achieving the easy victory it had gambled on.

The MiG engagements of September brought the total of US aircraft lost to this cause to eighteen since the start of the invasion. The NVNAF would claim sixty-seven kills by the end of the air war, whereas the US fighter squadrons were credited with a total of 137. It was widely believed at the time that this last estimate was conservative, although until an official list is put out by Vietnam, just how well the US airmen did in air-to-air combat will remain an unanswered question. It became increasingly obvious that fighting with missiles brought great problems in verification of kills; both Sparrows and Sidewinders were subject to erratic flight paths, and there were numerous instances of both missile and MiG disappearing into cloud. If, as was often the case, the overcast extended all the way to ground level and aircraft and missile came together, the result could easily remain unseen by either side.

Rogue missiles could be a hazard to friendly forces,

too. An incident occurred on 16 April that involved the US guided-missile cruiser Worden (CG 18) becoming a target for a stray antiradiation missile. It struck the ship out in the Gulf of Tonkin, causing one death and nine wounded.

Another strike on Phuce Yen, Yen Bai, Quang Land, and Vinh airfields took place on 30 September, the bombs destroying five MiGs and damaging nine on the ground. This represented about ten percent of the tactical force then available to the NVNAF.

October was a month of intense air activity, a period when, among other units, the 67th TFS from Korat flew a proportion of the 460 sorties it was to complete with the Weasel F-4C. On 7 October, there were three hundred sorties to targets in the North, and at least 370 on the 16th. The rate dropped to 220 on 21 October but rose again to 313 by TAC aircraft, plus 23 by the B-52s, on the 29th, all the BUFF sorties being on targets below the 20th parallel. By then Linebacker I had officially ended, and the peace talks had resumed again. Aircrews hardly noticed any slicing up of the calendar into the end or beginning of phases of combat, for there were always missions into Laos if the North was briefly off limits for another period. Heavy raids were made on targets in Laos and Cambodia on 1 November, the day after Korat witnessed the deactivation of the 469th TFS.

The base had seen further changes in Air Force occupancy, not only with new squadrons but new aircraft. By 16 October, the 354th TFW with its A-7Ds went fully operational. The snub-nosed Vought attack bomber rapidly built up a fine reputation for its ordnance-carrying capability. It was tough and reliable, and one thing that endeared the "Little Hummer" to pilots was its heavy armor protection. This was very welcome in the dangerous skies of SE Asia, and among other attributes, this good survivability record enabled the A-7 to take over the exacting task of Sandy cover for the rescue of downed aircrew.

The reliable old "Spad," the AD Skyraider, flew its last rescue support mission on 7 November, and later that month, its successor was to demonstrate just how able it was to perform this mission. Before that, on the 15th, TAC mounted one of the heaviest series of strikes on North Vietnamese targets. The sortie rate reached 800 as the fighter bombers sought out transportation, storage, and defensive sites in the southern panhandle area.

The following day, the 561st TFS lost another F-105G—which turned out to be the last Thud loss of the war. Fortunately for the crew, they were not destined to become the last F-105 POWs of the war, thanks largely to Major Colin A. "Arnie" Clarke.

Bobbin 1 had been part of a Korat force supporting an Arc Light strike in RP III when it had been shot down by a SAM. Both crewmen elected and landed in dense underbrush in a valley near Thanh Hoa. For two days they evaded the NVA, many of whom were manning AAA and SAM sites in the area. They were in voice contact with Sandy A-7s using their hand radio bleepers, but there seemed little chance of a successful rescue under the very noses of the enemy. Arnie Clarke was determined to try.

Apart from the proximity of forces lethal to a helicopter, the weather all but prevented the HH-53 landing. Clarke kept searching for a gap in the overcast, which was at least hiding the would-be rescuers—for a while, at least. When the rescue force attempted a way in from another direction, Sandy I narrowly missed being shot down. Remaining on station far longer than was healthy, Clarke continued to search for a clear landing zone for the Jolly Greens. He had been airborne for nearly seven hours, and the second pair of helos were critically low on fuel. Clarke sent them home and called in the original pair, while seeking out a tanker to top off his own tanks.

Finally, a CH-53 did land. Clarke and other A-7 pilots kept the AAA crews' heads down, and the pickup was finally made. The tenacious A-7 pilot took hits on his aircraft during strafing passes on the enemy guns, and he diverted to Da Nang rather than risk limping back to Korat. His nine-hour marathon sortie earned Clarke one of the most deserved Air Force Crosses of the Vietnam war.

It was missions like that, plus an impressive showing over the battlefield, that made the A-7 a star performer during the last phases of the air war. The 354th managed to participate in combat operations during the two Linebacker operations that finally ended the war against North Vietnam.

Bad weather in November saw a decrease of TAC sorties, and on the 30th, only forty had flown. But overall, the total was rising. A weather improvement during the first week of December saw another surge during the four days of the 7th to the 10th. B-52s flew 242 sorties while TAC aircraft put up a maximum effort over the South, with 426 in two days, plus 150 to northern targets in the same period. Another 323 were achieved in the South on 12–13 December, the B-52s attacking a column estimated to contain at least a hundred tanks plus troops coming down the Trail. Heavy rain over the area cut TAC sorties to just twenty on 13 December.

North Vietnam was still unwilling to agree to a satisfactory cease-fire by mid-month, and Nixon finally unleashed the B-52s on the heart of the late Uncle Ho's empire. On 18 December, the big bombers initiated Linebacker II. The night bombing of Hanoi began early that evening when 129 B-52s released their loads on Hoa Lac airfield, fifteen miles west of the city center. Unseen by the SAC crews were the support forces, which numbered thirty-nine on this first mission. They comprised F-4s carrying out the triple duties of chaff bombing, chaff escort, and B-52 escort, with Iron Hand F-105Gs and EB-66s/handling ECM and anti-SAM tasks. Throughout Linebacker II, tactical aircraft would release 126 tons of chaff to create blinding "snowstorms" across enemy radar screens, hiding the true size and direction of the bomber waves. The Korat Weasels were then under the command of Colonel Richard E. Markling, who had replaced Stanley Umstead on 5 August.

On each B-52 strike during what became known as the "eleven-day war," the support formations had their work cut out to protect the bombers, which were, by TAC standards, extremely slow. And by having to fly much lower, flights engaged on chaff flights ran an enormous risk. To lay an effective chaff screen, flights had to adopt a steady, straight, and level run, and escorting them became a very unpopular pastime. Nobody wanted to fly over North Vietnam at anything less than maximum speed and, of course, the enemy soon got wise to the reason why chaff flights were not doing so.

The enemy also began to integrate its defense system; AAA fire could not reach the B-52s, and it was left to the SAMs, in concert with the MiG force, to protect the homeland. The latter, however, failed almost totally to penetrate the escort. Two MiG-21s that did so were promptly shot down by B-52 tail gunners. SAMs were, therefore, the main danger. A pilot on one of the early missions commented that he'd seen "wall-to-wall SAMs" aimed at the bombers, and this situation continued. It was to the credit of the Weasel crews that the loss rate of fifteen B-52s was not any higher; evidence of the F-105/F-4 hunter-killer teams' work was reflected in SAMs being launched like Fourth of July fireworks, often despite the fact that their radar guidance was destroyed or shut down.

As the Linebacker strikes reached a peak over the Christmas 1972 period, so the NVA ground to a halt in South Vietnam. Nixon called off the bombers on 29 December, and by the end of the month the enemy was at a standstill. This time, it really did look like peace was at hand. Whether or not the North Vietnamese really were "bombed back to the conference table," as was widely believed, they did finally agree to the terms of a cease-fire.

It had taken TAC 51,000 sorties to bring about the necessary conditions for friendly ground forces to push the invaders back. In flying those missions, 124,000 tons of munitions were released over the battlefronts by US aircraft alone. And it was not over yet. In what can be termed the post-Linebacker "mopping up" phase that took up most of January 1973, strike aircraft were far from idle. Following the last air combats with the MiGs, during which the final Air Force and Navy kills were made on 8 and 12 December, respectively, tactical squadrons entered an intensive round of missions between 17 and 25 January in which another 3,000 sorties or so were flown. Even while US aircraft were pounding the enemy, an announcement that a cease-fire was imminent was made on 23 January. Four days before the end of the month, the cease-fire was finally signed.

But it was February before a cease-fire was to bring an end to the war in Laos—at least as far as the US Tactical Air Command was concerned—and mid-April before all air operations over that troubled area ended. In the meantime, North Vietnam at least complied with one of the terms of the cease-fire—the release of all US POWs. The first batch was welcomed back between 12 and 27 January, and the balance, bringing the total to 587 men, by 29 March. This move convinced many Americans that the war in SE Asia was finally over. Unfortunately, that was far from true.

Understandably, there was pressure to bring the squadrons home after the war in Vietnam had "ended," and it was not long before local US commanders were hard put to meet the ongoing sortie requirements to support friendly troops in Cambodia, and when required, cover rescue forces to extract downed airmen. Part of the difficulty faced by Colonel Mele Vojvodich, who took command of the 388th on 25 January 1973, was that the Stateside squadrons were at Korat only on a TDY basis, and tended to run things as they would under TAC guidelines at home. PACAF wanted, preferably, a PCS—permanent change of station—for the 354th, or its own squadron of A-7s to complete the job the 388th was in

Thailand to do. The trouble was that few people knew how long it was going to take.

In the event, the 388th got its A-7D unit, the 3rd TFS, by March. It was activated at Korat on the 15th of that month, with Lieutenant Colonel Edward "Moose" Skowron in command. Thus freed from pilot rotations outside its control, the 388th could continue Sluf operations over Cambodia and ensure that the important Sandy mission could be maintained by pilots familiar with the operational area. It was well known that you didn't, if at all possible, give this mission to someone fresh from outside the theater, for rescues were demanding, often violent affairs involving low-level delivery of ordnance, sometimes ground strafing, and equally often, the necessity to remain on station over the hapless aircrew member's position for what seemed like an eternity, awaiting the rescue helos.

On the positive side, there were very few people who had anything but praise for the Vought A-7. "Sluf" quickly came into the same category as "Thud" had for the F-105. It was a term of affection, not the opposite. To many eyes, it was an ugly aircraft, but that meant next to nothing to a pilot tasked to hit a very small target probably close to "friendlies" in less-than-ideal weather conditions, or to spot the tiny pinpoint of a parachute in miles of hostile jungle. Soon the term Sluf driver, coupled with Sandy, came to mean raw courage of a high order.

Small-arms fire could be just as dangerous over Cambodia as the heavier stuff had been over North Vietnam: a hit was just that, irrespective of what had made it. If it disabled the aircraft, the result was often a very heavy glider that had to be put down, and fast.

One such case occurred on 4 May, when the 3rd TFS carried out a ground attack mission against boat traffic. Coming off target, 1/Lt Thomas Dickens, flying A-7D call sign Philco 3, was hit. The small-arms fire found a vital spot, and the engine promptly quit. Dickens ejected, to be quickly picked up by the ubiquitous Jolly Green Giant.

But by the early summer, time was running out for the war that never seemed to end. On 1 July, the law that cut off all funding "to finance directly or indirectly combat activities by US military forces in or over or from off the shores of South Vietnam, Laos or Cambodia" was signed by Richard Nixon. That about said it all, and on the morning of 15 August 1973 a 354th TFW A-7 returned to Korat after dropping the last US bombs of the Southeast Asian war.

Relieved to hear the news, the men of the 388th soon realized that they would not be going home. The Wing remained in Thailand, flying training missions. Asia was still in turmoil, and an end to US air operations did not mean that peace reigned except, as irony would have it, in North Vietnam.

While the world rapidly tried to forget recent events in the region, US airmen continued to fly, sweating out their eventual return home. The 17th WWS had flown its last Iron Hand mission at the end of the Linebacker II campaign, on 29 December 1972. And although the Thud had stayed in the theater until mid-1973, the 561st flying its final sorties on 3 August shortly before its departure for home, the remaining craft were now more urgently required in the US for crew training. That still left the 17th in place at Korat, and this squadron was not destined to leave until the fall of 1974.

The end of the US combat involvement did not, therefore, see anything like a mass exodus from Korat. In August, the flightline held about seventy-five A-7Ds of the 388th's 3rd TFS and the 354th TFW, and the latter continued its TDY rotations until 23 May 1974, the Wing retaining a "split" status and supporting tactical elements at both Korat and itsobase, Myrtle Beach, South Carolina. The 3rd TFS was itself a part of the 388th until 15 December 1975.

Events outside the borders of Thailand continued to be a focus of media attention whenever it appeared that the fragile status quo would be broken. An ongoing Air Force presence in the region meant numerous transport and liaison flights, while fighter pilots completed their tours of overseas duty. For the most part these were not operational sorties, despite the closeness of armed forces that remained poised to fulfill long-standing military objectives under various political creeds.

Since March 1973, MACV headquarters had been at Nakhom Phenom, and with the release of the remaining POWs, the last US military support personnel left South Vietnam. Those combat operations that remained to be flown were therefore directed from Thailand for more than two years. With the end of the bombing of Cambodia on 14 August, there remained little more than reconnaissance and military supply flights throughout the region, although there were frequent violations of the cease-fire in South Vietnam. While TAC fighter bombers remained on station, there were more changes of base as the US slimmed down its air assets in the region for the last time.

On 15 March of the following year, the 42nd TEWS was reassigned when its attachment to the 388th ended. The unit had been on nonoperational status since 17 January. In July, the 347th TFS detached part of the 428th/429th TFS element in the theater to Korat, four days before the last 8th TFW flight was made from Ubon. The 347th Wing was then equipped with the F-111A, and although the type had previously visited Korat, this was the first time that the potent fighter bomber had been based there. The detachment was to last until 30 June 1975.

In a busy month for Korat, the 19th saw the C-130s of the 16th Special Operation Squadron arrive for another spell of TDY, which would not end until 8 December 1975.

It was 16 September before the 8th Wing finally left Ubon, its F-4s headed for Kunsan AB, Korea. Home plate was the destination of the last F-105G to depart, an event that occurred on 29 October. As with Korat, Ubon remained open. For another nine months or so, the base would have an American presence, albeit a small one.

It was not long before the cease-fire in South Vietnam was being regularly violated, and evidence was forthcoming of another Communist buildup in the North. By law, the US was prevented from flying missions of a direct ''military involvement'' nature.

When it finally broke, the North Vietnamese invasion of the South was far from unexpected. With a more than two-year breathing space, which enabled ample repair of installations wrecked in the Linebacker campaigns, the North Vietnamese estimated that a ''second try'' to remove the country's divisions would be successful. They also knew that the repeal of the Tonkin Gulf Resolution would not bring US aircraft back over the battlefield. Also, their estimate of the strength of South Vietnamese will to hold on to an ostensibly democratic existence must have been far more than just guesswork. They would surely have known that without US support the South's will to fight was at best patchy and at worst, nonexistent.

And so it was to prove. When the North captured an entire South Vietnamese province in January 1975, even its leaders were surprised at the speed at which this was achieved. That is not to say that the South offered no resistance, but the lack of a cohesive military policy, bad communications, and the sheer size of the territory to be defended all but sealed the fate of the South. By early April, with chaotic conditions throughout the country, refugees choking the roads, many of whom were soldiers who had abandoned their weapons and fled, President Gerald Ford was obliged to implement a military airlift for those US personnel still in the country, as well as key Vietnamese officials, whose fate at the hands of the victors of the war was uncertain.

As the death throes of South Vietnam unfolded in the world's press, the Khymer Rouge threatened Phnom Penh. The US ambassador and his staff left the capital beginning on 12 April, the evacuation being completed on the 16th, the day before the capital fell. Less than a week later, South Vietnam's president Thieu resigned to be replaced by Duong Van Minh. The end was then near, and Operation Frequent Wind began at the end of April.

The massive evacuation of Saigon—the largest ever to be undertaken by helicopters—brought the TAC squadrons in Thailand to their highest alert state since the cease-fire in the South. While there was no likelihood that the Americans would participate in the war per se, sorties were flown to guard the evacuation. In the event, no incidents took place before Minh announced the unconditional surrender of his country on 30 April.

Being obliged to stand by and watch South Vietnam fall, many Americans close to the staggering events of the past weeks could only scratch their heads and wonder what in hell Rolling Thunder, Linebacker, and all the rest of the combat operations flown in the last ten years or so had been about, if this was the way it was being allowed to end. The phrase "all for nought" aptly summed up the incredible effort the US had made to bring off a solution other than the one that was unfolding less than one hour's flying time away.

One last alert was to come. On 12 May, the Khymer Rouge seized the US container ship *Mayaguez* in the Gulf of Siam. The Cambodian force did not respond to diplomatic moves to have the vessel's thirty-nine-man crew released immediately, and on the 14th, a rescue operation was initiated. In case of trouble, Korat launched a number of A-7 and F-111 sorties to prevent countermoves by Khymer forces, two F-111s making the first runs over the ship to verify its position, on the afternoon of 13 May. They found the *Mayaguez* anchored off Koh Tang island. Subsequent relays of 3rd TFS A-7Ds and AC-130 gunships kept an eye on developments, the latter maintaining night patrols. When surveillance aircraft were fired on from the shoreline and Khymer gunboats, the fire was not returned, not at first.

Warning shots were fired to prevent any boats reaching the mainland with the pirated vessel's crew and cargo. One fishing boat did manage to land the crew in Cambodia before ferrying the men to another island, where they were held until their release.

During the daylight hours of the 14th, tactical aircraft sank a number of Khymer gunboats before the AC-130s came back that night. No satisfactory terms for the release of the *Mayaguez* could be established, and the US then decided on a combined USAF/Marines assault to effect a rescue.

Getting the helo-borne Marines in (and out) proved to be quite a tricky operation, and the Air Force was called upon to lay down suppressive fire to prevent the enemy from interfering with the choppers. The 388th's aircraft saw out the SE Asian war to the bitter end as far as combat was concerned, for it was the aircraft of the 3rd TFS that maintained an FAC A-7 over the beach area and called in relays of Slufs to draw fire and thus destroy enemy guns. It was a hard task, as the Khymers kept their heads down when the FAC was in range, not wanting to draw fire from the prowling A-7s.

In a day packed with action, including the dropping of riot-control gas by the A-7s and further strafing attacks on gunboats, the rescue was finally accomplished with the help of further rocket, bomb, and strafing attacks from Air Force F-4s. Some fourteen hours of hectic activity resulted in the *Mayaguez* proceeding on its way under the command of its crew, none of whom were harmed in the operation.

The F-4 made its last operational, noncombat flight in SE Asia on 29 May, and the following June the 6233rd Air Base Squadron packed its bags and in a small ceremony, hauled down the flag at Ubon. The F-111s of the 347th TFW bid adieu to Korat on the 30th and the only tactical combat aircraft remaining on the base were then the A-7s of the 3rd TFS.

It was 28 November before the 388th TFW was advised that operations would cease after the last training flight of the day, and almost another month before the Wing itself completed its long stay at Korat. The 16th SOS left the wing on 8 December.

The 388th was bound for a new home in the US, namely Hill AFB, Utah. Flying F-4Ds, the wing began operations on 15 March 1976, having begun to receive aircraft in January.

Phantoms remained with the 388th until when what many believed to be one of the Air Force's hottest fighters, the diminutive F-16, arrived. The 388th was then part of the 12th Air Force and had four squadrons of F-16As with some two-seat B models for conversion training, these being the 4th, 16th, 34th, and 421st TFS.

During its last years in Thailand, the 388th had been led by Mele Vojvoditch, who handed over command to Colonel Robert K. Crouch on 1 July, and on 3 January 1974, Colonel Thomas H. Normile became the CO. His period of command ended on 2 July, when Colonel John P. Russell took up the reins and led until 10 July 1975.

Colonel Neil L. Eddins was in command when the wing finally left Thailand, and his tenure was to last until well into the Stateside period, with Colonel Robert L. Rodee taking over on 19 April 1977. He remained in the hot seat until 2 August that year, when the 388th command passed to Colonel Davis C. Rohr on 3 August 1977.

When the 388th departed, Korat reverted to Royal Thai Air Force jurisdiction under its Thai name of Nakhorn Ratchasima. The base was occupied by No. 1 Wing RTAF with three jet squadrons, two of Northrop F-5s, and one of T-33 trainers. Although many of the buildings were no longer needed and some were pulled down or allowed to fall into disrepair, much evidence of the base's former tenants is visible today. The tall water tower en route to the old club is still there, as are a number of Quonset huts. The swimming pool, now a bit choked with weeds, may possibly have a rusting motor scooter lying in the deep end. A couple of scooters are known to have ended up in the pool after parties.

A veteran strolling around the huge base—the Thais occupy only a relatively small area of it—would see plenty of evidence of the old 388th, including the Wing's number painted on flaking hut walls and marking out officers' parking in the headquarters area.

As of the late 1980s, Korat was still occupied by elements of No. 1 Wing, including a squadron of F-16s. Visiting USAF units fly with the Thais on exercises such as Cobra Gold. Occasionally, although the problem is played down, there is evidence that this part of SE Asia is still not entirely free of strife. Thailand has had border disputes with Laos, and a number of aircraft have been damaged as a result.

If the buildings and general surroundings fail to jog the memory of anyone who was at Korat during the Vietnam War years, there is something else. In front of the club there is a modest memorial to one of the smallest members of the old 388th. A simple stone bears the name "Roscoe." This was the pooch that showed up on the base one day during 1965 and just sort of adopted the men of the Wing. Roscoe was part of the Korat scene for some ten years before he passed away on 13 September 1975. Part of the dedication to him reads, "I spent all my life waiting for my master, but he never returned from North Vietnam . . ."

Representative Aircraft, 388th TFW

F-105Ds:

Serial	Name(s)	Sqn(s)	Remarks
58-1150	Cobra	34th	w/o 26 June 68
58-1152/JJ	Miss Mary/Das Jaeger/Arkansas Razorback	421st/34th	
58-1154		44th	w/o 3 Aug 67
58-1156		421st	
58-1157	Bubbles I/Shirley Ann	13th/421st/ 44th	w/o 3 Jan 68
58-1167	Miss Universe	34th	
58-1169	Dragon Jane	34th/469th	w/o 5 Oct 67
58-1170		44th	w/o 10 Nov 67
58-1172	The Stud Thud	13th	
59-1727	The Great Pumpkin II	469th	w/o 3 Sept 67
59-1737	Cherry Boy	469th	w/o 11 Jan 66
59-1743	Darn Dago/ Arkansas Traveler	13th	
59-1749	Mr. Toad/Marilee E	469th	w/o 23 Sept 67
59-1739	Rum Runner	34th	
59-1750	Flying Anvil	469th	w/o 14 Dec 67
59-1752	Yankee Sky Dog	13th	w/o 23 Aug 67
59-1760/JJ	War Lord II	34th	w/o Apr 77

F-105Ds:

Serial	Name(s)	Sqn(s)	Remarks
59-1759	Miss Carol/Short Picture	44th	
59-1771/JV	Ohio Express/Foley's Folly	469th	
60-0409	Bunny Baby	469th	w/o 31 May 68
60-0421	The Great Pumpkin	469th	w/o 14 May 67
60-0422	The Red Baron	469th	w/o 17 Dec 67
60-0423	Sexy Sheila/Butterfly Bomber	44th	
60-0424	Mickey Titti Chi	34th	w/o 10 July 67
60-0425		44th	w/o 17 Oct 67
60-0428	Pollyana	44th	w/o 19 Sept 68
60-0430		44th	w/o 7 Nov 67
60-0458	Herr Kleines Mans	469th	
60-0434	Damn you Charlie Brown	13th/44th	w/o 9 Oct 67
60-0435/JJ		34th	w/o 28 Nov 69
60-0436/JJ		34th	w/o 25 Apr 68
60-0445	Entropy Machine	44th	
60-0444		44th	w/o 7 Oct 67
60/0449/JJ	Bounty Hunter	34th	
60-0462	The Huntress	34th	w/o 26 Mar 68
60-0458			
60-0482/JV		469th	
60-0488	The Virgin	44th	
60-0494	Mr. Pride	469th	w/o 2 July 67
60-0464/JV	Dee Dee II	469th	
60-0497	Miss T	44th	w/o 18 Nov 67
60-0505	Fighting Irishman	13th/34th	w/o 18 Feb 69
60-0512	The Mercenary	34th	w/o 1 Sept 68

F-105Ds:

Serial	Name(s)	Sqn(s)	Remarks
60-0518/JE	Thud Protector of SEA/Billie Babe	469th	w/o 15 July 69
60-0530	Tandem Turtle	34th	w/o 16 June 69
60-5376	Valiante	34th	
60-5381/JV		469th	w/o 14 June 69
61-0055	Dorothy II	469th	w/o 8 June 68
61-0068	Barbara E	469th	w/o 5 Jan 68
61-0069	Pussy Galore/ Cherry Girl	44th/469th	
61-0078	Sittin' Pretty	469th	w/o 3 Sept 67
61-0124	Eight Ball	34th	w/o 20 Nov 67
61-0152/JJ	Eight Ball	34th	
61-0126	Ol' Red Jr.	469th	w/o 27 Oct 67
61-0132/JJ	Hanoi Special	34th	w/o 14 May 68
61-0161/JV	The Outlaw	469th	
61-0194	The Avenger	34th	w/o 28 May 68
61-0197/JV		469th	w/o 14 Aug 66
61-0205	Mr. Blackbird/The Liquidator	34th	w/o 17 Oct 67
61-0206		469th/34th	w/o 15 Apr 68
61-0208	Blitzkrieg	34th	w/o 19 Nov 67
61-0213	Shady Lady	13th	w/o 15 June 67
61-0219	Linda Lou/The Traveler	469th	w/o 17 Aug 68
61-0220	I Dream of Jeannie	469th	w/o 15 Apr 70
62-4221	The Fighting Irishman/Wild Child	13th/34th	w/o 18 Nov 67
62-4248	Lady Luck	34th	w/o 74
62-4264/JJ	Rompin' Rudy	34th	w/o 27 Oct 68
62-4269/JV	Okie Jody	469th	

F-105Ds:

Serial	Name(s)	Sqn(s)	Remarks
62-4242/JV		469th	
62-4270/JJ		34th	
62-4273		44th	w/o 17 Aug 67
62-4283	Miss Mi Nookie	44th	w/o 18 Nov 67
62-4286	The Mad Bomber	469th	w/o 6 Nov 67
62-4316		469th	w/o 30 June 67
62-4326		44th	w/o 17 Oct 67
62-4346/JV	Good Golly Miss Molly	469th	
62-4352	Thunderchief	34th	w/o 5 May 67
62-4356			w/o 28 Oct 67
62-4387	Eve of Destruction	34th	
62-4359	12 O'Clock High	44th	
62-4361/JE	War Wagon	44th	
62-4395	Emily	44th	w/o 5 Apr 67
62-4401	The Flying Dutchman	469th	w/o 5 May 67

F-105F/G:

Serial	Name(s)	Sqn(s)	Remarks
62-4424/JE	Crown Seven	44th	w/o 11 May 72
62-4430			w/o 5 Nov 67
62-4435/JE		44th	w/o 14 May 69
62-4416	Little Stevie	13th	
62-4428/JE	Rum Runner/June Bug	44th	
62-4435/JE	Roman Knight	44th	
62-4446	Sneaky Pete	13th	
63-8274/JE	The Great Speckled Bird	44th	

F-105F/G:

Serial	Name(s)	Sqn(s)	Remarks
63-8289/JE		44th	w/o 12 May 67
63-8284/JE		44th	
63-8295	Mugly Other	13th	w/o 18 Nov 67
63-8289	Sam Dodger	13th	
63-8312			w/o 29 Feb 68
63-8275/JE	Bonnie and Clyde	44th	w/o 29 Sept 72
63-8302/JE	The Jefferson Airplane/The Smith Brothers/Cough Drop Special	13th	
63-8304/WW	Mad German Express	561st	
63-8312		13th	
63-8317	Half Fast	13th	
63-8319/JE	Sam Seeker	44th	
63-8329/JE	The Protester's Protector	44th	w/o 28 Jan 70
63-8330			w/o 7 Oct 67
63-8353		13th	w/o 15 July 68
63-8356	Miss Molly		w/o 5 Jan 68
63-8327/JE		44th	
63-8291/JB		17th	

F-4E Phantom:

Serial	Name(s)	Sqn(s)	Remarks
66-0380/JJ	Diane	34th	w/o 3 Jan 71
67-0208/JJ	Here Come the Judge	34th	
67-0214/JJ		34th	w/o 25 Apr 70
67-0219/JJ		34th	w/o 11 Nov 69

F-4E Phantom:

Serial	Name(s)	Sqn(s)	Remarks
67-0230/JJ	Can-Do!	34th	
67-0261/JJ	Okie	34th	w/o 9 Aug 69
67-0269/JJ		34th	
67-0275/JJ	Sweetie Pie	34th	
67-0277/JJ		34th	w/o 1 July 72
67-0279/JJ	Tiny Bubbles/The Wrecking Crew	34th	w/o 30 June 70
67-0286/JV		469th	w/o 25 Jan 69
67-0283/JV		469th	
67-0287/JV	Positive Thinker	469th	
67-0288/JV	Arkansas Traveler II	469th	
67-0290/JV		469th	
67-0293/JV		469th	w/o 7 May 70
67-0295/JV		469th	w/o 9 June 70
67-0296/JJ		34th	w/o 5 July 72
67-0299/JV		469th	
67-0300/JV		469th	w/o 5 Dec 69
67-0301/JV/ JJ	Honey Bucket	469th/34th	
67-0303/JJ/ JV		34th/469th	w/o 8 June 72
67-0306/JV	War Lover	469th	
67-0308/JV	Betty Lou	469th	
67-0309/JV	Eltoro Bravo	469th	
67-0311/JV	Fightin' Irish	469th	
67-0313/JJ	Spunky VI	34th	
67-0315/JV	Aggressor	469th	
67-0322/JV	Little Chris	469th	
67-0339/JJ		34th	w/o 5 July 72
67-0342/JJ	Li'l Buddha	34th	

F-4E Phantom:

Serial	Name(s)	Sqn(s)	Remarks
67-0392/JV		469th	
68-0313/JJ		34th	
69-0276/JJ		34th	w/o 12 Oct 72
68-0468/JJ		34th	
69-7551/JV		469th	

F-4D:

65-0608